Slanted

H. L. Wegley

Romantic Suspense

Cover Design: Samantha Fury
http://www.furycoverdesign.com/

ISBN-13: 978-1-732763678
ISBN-10: 1732763674

Also available in eBook publication

OTHER BOOKS BY H. L. WEGLEY

Against All Enemies Series
1 Voice in the Wilderness
2 Voice of Freedom
3 Chasing Freedom

Pure Genius Series
1 Hide and Seek
2 On the Pineapple Express
3 Moon over Maalaea Bay
4 Triple Threat

Witness Protection Series
1 No Safe Place
2 No True Justice
3 No Turning Back

Stand-Alone Books
Virtuality
The Janus Journals

DEDICATION

The hero of *Slanted*, Hunter Jones, is a data scientist who seeks to expose the use of Internet search-engines for nefarious purposes. *Slanted* is dedicated to the real-world data scientists who tackle big data problems, not simply to maximize profits for some business enterprise, but for the benefit of all mankind. I cannot name them all here, but I'm referring to scientists like Dr. Kira Radinsky, who predicts disease outbreaks and other events with global impacts. We need these people with big minds and big hearts who can wield the tools to tame big data for the benefit of everyone.

CONTENTS

ACKNOWLEDGMENTS

Thanks to my wife, Babe, for listening to me read the story to her three times and for catching several mistakes.

How do you create a cover that portrays suspense and Internet bias in a remote, forest setting? Thank you, Samantha Fury, for solving that conundrum with your cover design.

Thanks to my sister-in-law, Duke Gibson, for her willingness to read another draft to help me determine if this story was working.

Thanks, Gail Ostheller, for going above and beyond by trying to proof the story though you were dealing with health problems.

Many thanks to Dr. Robert Epstein for his research and for sharing his concerns about the influence of the Internet on the thinking of many Americans.

I also want to thank two photographers who made their work available to license for cover development. Gemphotography provided the photo of the lady running through the forest and AlohaHawaii provided the photo of the young girl running that Samantha Fury used to represent little Samantha in the story.

Though my words seem to be in shorter supply these days, I thank my Lord and Savior for leaving me enough of them to write another story.

These six things the Lord hates,
Yes, seven are an abomination to Him:
A proud look,
A lying tongue,
Hands that shed innocent blood,
A heart that devises wicked plans,
Feet that are swift in running to evil,
A false witness who speaks lies,
And one who sows discord among brethren.

Proverbs 6:16-19 (NKJV)

Prologue

"Do I want to rule the world? Let me think about that for a minute." James Bratkowski, CEO and founder of IT giant, Q-It, paused and studied the beaming face of his Vice President of Product Development, Andy Rosenberg.

If he didn't answer soon, Andy, like an excited puppy, would either hyperventilate or wet his pants. This project was Andy's brainchild and, as such—

"Well, do you or don't you? The algorithm's done. Two weeks ago, I showed you the design that my data scientists engineered. We can implement this, on-the-fly, worldwide, without disrupting our search engine. And, when it's done—"

"I know. I get to rule the world."

"That's a bit of hyperbole for effect. And since nobody will know that you're the emperor, you—"

"Emperor? I want to be the emperor who keeps his clothes on, and I don't want my clothes morphing into an orange jumpsuit."

Andy blasted out a breath of frustration. "No one can prove what we're doing. We're just giving people what they want, distilling the data down to the finest—"

"Distilling, that's a good analogy. What you really mean is we're getting them intoxicated on whatever type of spirits we decide to serve. Tell me again—a simple overview—how do the data and algorithm work together? And how do they achieve our goals, political and financial?"

Andy took a deep breath, settled into his chair, and clasped his hands on the corner of Jim's desk. "This is a highly simplified description of what we're doing. We add to our database schema some fields to indicate which area of interest a bit of data—a news article, a book, a post, a picture—belongs to. With that, we add a descriptor of the relative importance to that area—areas such as an election, a political issue, a natural disaster, economic news, or a crime. Note that we can add areas of interest anytime we want simply by re-indexing the data." Andy paused.

"Now, when our customers search for something, we order the data returned to them by its relative importance as we have defined it. We can even choose what levels of importance should *not* be displayed in the query results." Andy stopped, obviously waiting for feedback.

"So over time, Q-It's customers' opinions would be shaped by the information they see ... or don't see?"

"Exactly, and you become the emperor of your global empire."

"Suppose some sore loser in an election goes to the DOJ, and they come after me with an orange suit?"

"Jim, you were only trying to tame a beastly data problem by giving users what they most wanted to see."

"But we're biasing the query results. We've slanted everything."

"Unintentionally, of course."

"Then, Andy, we need to put some verbal policies in place specifying that we shall never document any instructions for how we assign priorities to the data."

"Don't worry about that. Priorities are built into the algorithm. They're not contained in policies or procedures that people follow. Investigators would need to analyze the algorithm, reverse-engineer it and, if they did, they would conclude the biases were algorithmic and thus unintentional. The emperor will still be wearing his jeans and his no tuck shirt."

"In that case, maybe I do want to rule the world. But, Andy?"

"Yes." Andy was practically bouncing in his seat from excitement.

"Restrict all knowledge of what we're actually doing to the minimum set of people required. No one should know everything, and all policies and procedures are spoken, repeated as necessary, but never documented. Do you understand?"

Andy stood and grinned. "I understand, your Imperial Majesty."

Chapter 1

Three years later

This interview might blow up in your face, dude.

Hunter Jones's right foot tapped out a snappy rhythm on the floor of the studio while he tried to shove the vexing thought from his mind.

Radio host, Zach Tanner, fiddled with his headphones, twisted knobs, and moved sliders on an impressive looking mixing console. "Are you ready to do this, Hunter?"

Was it wise to introduce his research in a live radio interview—to state that the biggest search engine on the planet was run by some corrupt people trying to steal people's autonomy and possibly an election? But surely there wouldn't be any real danger from the interview.

Some bright boys from MIT ran the company he was about to implicate. They were not members of organized crime. No one would kill him for his accusations. Lawsuits and injunctions, on the other hand ...

"Zach to Hunter. Where did you go? You ready, buddy?"

"I'm ready." His voice wasn't convincing, even to himself, and it drew a curious glance from Zach.

Hunter would be on the air live, albeit only to a local audience. And he did need to test the waters before he told the world about his research findings which could cause legal heck to break loose in the life of Hunter Jones.

Now he had Sam to consider. He couldn't afford to spend weeks or even days in court when he was the only stabilizing force in Sam's life. Eight-year-old Samantha had

had enough changes in these four months following her mother's death.

And her guardian, Hunter Jones, would not let the coming media storm or anything else upset Sam. If anyone attempted anything that hurt her in any way, Hunter would break their scrawny necks ... in the figurative sense, of course, unless—

"We're on in ten seconds." Zach adjusted Hunter's mic.

"We go live in 5, 4, 3, 2, 1—welcome to Zach's Facts, folks, factual news about significant events impacting Southern Oregon and the nation. My guest today is a personal friend, a genius with a heart and a conscience, Hunter Jones. You may not have heard about him before today, but I've got the feeling he's going to become a household name across America. Hunter, how are you doing on this fine June afternoon, the first day of summer?"

"I guess I'm a little nervous about this. It's my first time live on the air. But to an Edward R. Murrow graduate, like yourself, this is probably old hat ... about like me tearing into a one-hundred-terabyte data set."

"Speaking of big data, we've only got thirty minutes to cover your analysis of an incredible volume of data. Tell us what you analyze and what you're looking for?"

"I analyze your queries on the big search engines—your neighbors' searches, the whole nations' searches. And I look at the query results those searches return."

"Come on, you don't spy on all of your neighbors, do you?"

"Not personally. I don't associate any query with a particular person, only with the results it gets. I compare each query with all the results it could have returned and then look for any systematic prioritization of the returned data—you know, to see if certain types of information are given a significantly higher or lower priority in the query results. And I look to see if some potential results are never returned."

"What are we talking about, Hunter? Cheating? Lying to the public?"

"Let's not go there, Zach. We'll call it systematic bias, for now. It could be the result of the search algorithms. Maybe the specs weren't good, and they caused the programmers to inadvertently introduce biases when selecting the set of data and ordering it for the query results. And there are other non-malevolent possibilities for the biases I've seen."

"So you have seen biases?"

"I have."

"Which search engines have you analyzed?"

"Well, we all know the biggest by far is Q-It. I've looked at all the major search engines, but I've focused on Q-It."

"Tell us about Q-It's biases. How slanted is the information?"

Where was Zach going with this line of inquiry? They'd agreed that Zach wouldn't goad him like this. "I would rather complete my next phase of the research before—"

"Sounds like you *have* found some things that might interest our listeners?"

"I will let you know about that *after* my research report is written. I really would like to complete my research without court injunctions or lawsuits stopping me."

"Injunctions? Lawsuits? So there are nefarious findings about Q-It?"

"Zach, I didn't say that. And query results are only part of my analysis. For example, I've also found potential problems with all of the digital assistants. They record a lot of data that finds its way back to the search engine's data storage. That's inevitable when you have applications programmed to be your assistant and to respond to voice commands."

Zach was obviously trying to get under his skin. And it was working.

"So you wouldn't use any of the popular digital assistants?"

"I didn't say that." But Hunter had ventured beyond the point of no return. He might as well tell this local radio audience what was on his mind and try to gauge their reaction. If it was bad, at least they could try to limit the damage before the explosion went nationwide.

"Okay, tell us what you *did* say."

"Rather than tell you, I'm going to ask three questions. They should suffice. Question number one, do you really want human-coded software, spec'd out by a business enterprise, doing your thinking for you? Question number two, do you really think you'll get an undistorted view of reality if you allow that? Question number three, do you honestly believe that all the important facts will be provided in the query results you get from an Internet search engine? And here's a fourth question, surely no business enterprise would ever play politics with such troves of information ... would they?"

Zach's hand had hovered over a big red button on the console for the past four or five seconds. He pulled his hand back. "So, Hunter, you're insinuating that—"

"I'm not insinuating anything." If this is what Zach wanted from all his button pushing, he would get it. "I'm flat-out telling you, Zach. These people are lying to us in subtle ways by falsifying the evidence, slanting it in favor of their preferred conclusions and their preferred candidates. They can bend your mind, influence elections, and re-define truth if we let them."

Zach's hand moved toward the red button again, then stopped. "Thanks, Hunter ... folks, we've been live on the air with Hunter Jones who just expressed his *opinion* about Q-It and other Internet information gatherers. Now it's back to music on the Zach Tanner show." Zach hit the red button and turned off his mic.

"That wasn't my *opinion*, Zach. It was fact, and I have the data to prove it."

"But it was *my* opinion that you needed to cool off a bit, and I needed to end your diatribe before Q-It sics its attorneys on us. My boss probably won't be happy with the way things went before I shut down the interview."

"Then why were you trying to press all my buttons?"

"Sorry about that. I didn't mean to press the one that said detonate. But, after I did, I needed to call what you said '*your opinion*' for the time being. If I hadn't, I might've gotten myself fired, and then you would lose your local mouthpiece."

The studio door opened. "Zach?" A voice came from the hallway. "Zach ... uh, we weren't just local. Evidently, the network contacted Susan after reading the notice about the interview. They told her to turn you on nationwide."

"What? You just don't do that to someone who's—"

"In addition, she wanted your interview to be frank and spontaneous. Her words, not mine."

"Well, Mitch, that's what she got. So, whatever she thinks about what we just broadcasted, or about pulling my mic, or canning me, tell her this ... frankly, my dear, I don't give—"

"Now who needs to cool it, Zach." Hunter forced a laugh that had little mirth behind it.

Zach's furled brow said that he didn't see the humor.

But the truth of the matter was no one may be laughing after the feedback came from the news outlets and the pundits across America and after the network owners provided their input. And, certainly, not after they all got hauled into court by James Bratkowski, CEO of Q-It.

For Hunter Jones, the cat was definitely out of the bag. He had spilled the beans. Given away his secrets and— Hunter had run out of clichés to describe what he'd done.

He would have no control over which of the national punditocrats got first crack at his research. They would all hear about it now. And someone probably recorded the interview. Worst case, it might even be on YouTube tonight.

That's not how Hunter had planned to break his findings. And there would be unintended consequences from this interview gone awry.

Zach stood and pushed the door wide open. "You're free to go, Hunter. Right now, I need have to a little chat with Susan, my boss." Zach stopped when a tall, slender, middle-aged woman wearing a scowl rounded the hallway corner and headed his way.

Hunter stepped out of the studio doorway.

"Uncle Hunter ..." Samantha ran from the desk in the lobby, where the friendly receptionist had babysat Sam for the past half hour. Sam circled the approaching woman, nearly tripping her, then leaped into Hunter's arms.

He pulled the giggling eight-year-old to his chest. "Sam, how many times have I told you, I'm not your uncle."

"But you're not my dad, so ..."

Hunter stepped aside as the sour-faced woman, Zach's boss, strode by.

She shot him a glaring glance and then hurried into the studio.

Hunter and Sam needed to leave before they got splattered by whatever was about to hit the fan.

"That's right. I'm not your dad. I'm your guardian, Sam."

They walked down the hallway to the lobby of the radio station.

"You are such a *tool*. I can't call you guardian."

"Whatever that means. But if I'm a tool, can I be a variable speed, reversible drill?"

Her wrinkled nose said she wasn't going to comment on his interpretation of tool. "If I can't call you uncle, what am I supposed to call you?"

"First, you tell me what *tool* means, then we'll get to my official title."

Sam blasted out a sigh. "It means stupid."

"Doesn't fit, Sam. What's the latest word for cool or maybe awesome?"

"Dope." Sam grinned.

He clamped his hands on her waist and leaned Sam back to study her face.

That maneuver caused her boney little knees to poke painfully into his rib cage. "Dope? That ain't gonna work, either."

"Ain't ain't a word, Uncle Hunter." She rubbed her fingers over the stubble on his chin and wrinkled her nose again. "You need to shave."

While a loud discussion from somewhere behind him echoed down the hallway, Hunter set Sam down on the carpeted floor, curled his big hand around her tiny fingers, and walked out of the radio station into the warm Southern Oregon sunshine.

"Need to shave, huh? What do you expect? It's after four o'clock. Look. You're not gonna call me a dope, even if you say it means awesome, which I'm beginning to doubt. And I'm not your uncle, I'm your cousin, your second cousin. Got it, Sam?" He turned down the sidewalk toward his old Dodge pickup truck.

"Yeah, got'em both. But I could call you a goat."

"No, you're not calling me a goat. BTW, what does *goat* mean?"

"Greatest of all time. You could be my goat uncle."

He shook his head. "Here's the deal. Until we both decide on a good name for you to call me, I'm just Hunter. For us, Hunter means part dad, part uncle, and it means the person who loves you more than anybody in the whole world. Okay?"

She looked up at him, but Sam wasn't smiling. "Mama and dad love me more than anybody *not* in the whole world. So I guess you can be Hunter ... for now."

Sam's hand grew heavy the instant her shoulders drooped.

Hunter glanced down at the face now tilted down toward the sidewalk.

A track of glistening tears rolled down her tanned cheek.

Sam's dad, an Army Ranger, had been killed in Afghanistan two years ago. But her mom had died in an accident only four months ago, at the end of February. There were moments like this almost every day, though there was a little less crying now.

Hunter stopped, took a knee, and pushed her wavy blonde hair aside. He brushed the tears from Sam's cheeks. "Of all the people in heaven, your mom and dad love you the most. Well, God loves you that much too. But on this planet, Hunter loves you more than anybody. Got that?"

Two tiny arms circled his neck and nearly choked him. Sam might be small in stature, but she was strong in every sense of the word, body, mind and spirit. Much stronger than Hunter Jones.

When Sam released him, Hunter looked down into her perfectly sculpted face with the sprinkling of freckles across her nose. She was happiness on earth for Hunter Jones.

This was as good as God had allowed life to get for him. As much as he longed for adult companionship, life with this angelic imp would never be boring. But for an adult woman, life with a data geek like Hunter Jones would be the epitome of boring, even if the geek could run a sub-four-minute mile.

God knew what was best. For Hunter, it was Samantha Wilson.

Sam went silent for the fifteen-minute drive home. Her recovery time from a crying episode had shrunk to about fifteen minutes over the past couple of weeks. Odds were, in another two or three minutes, he wouldn't be able keep her quiet.

Hunter drove slowly down the long, graveled driveway to his modular home perched on the side of a small, oak-covered hill in Sams Valley, an unincorporated community a little northwest of Medford.

After he braked his truck to a stop in the circle drive, Sam popped her seatbelt and looked up at him. "I'm bored."

"School's only been out for three days. You can't be bored yet."

"Yes, I can. I'm bored out of my skeleton."

"You mean out of your skull."

"Out of my skull? I didn't say I was crazy, Uncle Hunter. Just bored. Can we take a vacation?"

Hunter slid out of his pickup and circled it to Sam's side.

She already had the door open.

He set her on the ground beside him. "How about I take you to Brookings next Saturday. We can spend the whole day on the beach. Tide pools, splashing in the waves ..."

"But we've done that before." Sam took his hand and led him to the front door. "I mean a *real* vacation."

"Let me think on it." He unlocked the door.

As he nudged Sam through the doorway, from the side pocket of his cargo shorts, his cell buzzed his leg. "Maybe we can have a real vacation after I finish my report."

Sam mumbled something about her best friend moving away.

Hunter pulled out his cell and glanced at the caller ID.

It displayed a 202 area code. Not a number in his contacts list.

The interview? Could someone already—not likely.

He answered.

"May I speak with Mr. Hunter Jones?" The words came wrapped in a deep, rich baritone that spoke softly, like someone trying to prevent anyone from hearing them.

Sam looked up at him and frowned. "Not again. More techie talk."

Hunter gave her the palms-out stop signal. "May I ask who is calling?"

"I take it that I'm speaking to Mr. Jones. This is Jeff Montgomery."

A DC area code. Jeff Montgomery. The name, like an electrical charge, zapped his memory. Hunter was speaking to President Gramm's Chief of Staff, Mr. Jeffrey Montgomery. "Yes, this is Hunter Jones."

"The Hunter Jones who was interviewed on the air about a half-hour ago?"

The fallout from going nuclear with Zach had begun, and it would be hotter than Bikini Atoll in March of 1954. That hydrogen bomb blast had vaporized three islands. What was President Gramm about to vaporize?

Come what may, he would not let this hurt Sam no matter what the president wanted.

Chapter 2

James Bratkowski, Q-It CEO and majority stock owner, looked out the window of his corner office and studied the building across the street.

It occupied an entire block a little north of downtown Seattle. The building held more storage capacity than the entire Internet had a few years ago.

Q-It was more than Jim's company. It had become a pathway to incredible power, provided he knew how to wield its influence in a smart, subtle manner.

A figure appeared in his open doorway, Andrew Rosenberg, one of the three senior VPs of the company. "Knock, Knock." His face held a scowl instead of the usual smile.

"What is it, Andy?" Jim motioned to the chair across from his desk.

"It's almost seven o'clock. I thought you might have gone home." Andy sat in the chair while his right foot bounced on the floor to a furious rhythm.

"Something's got you riled. What's up?"

Andy blew out a sharp breath. "One of my people spotted something that was just posted to YouTube a couple of hours ago. You need to see this, Jim."

"What happened? Server problems? Or is someone revealing our performance secrets?"

"Our secrets. You could say that, but it has nothing to do with our servers or their configuration."

Jim blew out his relief. With over eight-hundred thousand identical servers running world-wide, any systematic error required nearly a million fixes. The few times that had happened were nightmares that generated many sleepless nights. Thankfully, that was not the case here.

"So what's been posted to YouTube this time? Am I unfaithful to my new bride? Or are we expecting twins? Maybe both?"

"This isn't funny, your Imperial Majesty. You really do need to see it. Someone slapped together a slideshow with an audio track from a radio interview that ran live this afternoon."

Jim had a lot of potential enemies, but he couldn't think of any who would sink to a radio interview to attack him. They would have used television or social media. Besides, how big of an audience could a radio interview reach? But YouTube ...

Andy pointed to the monitor on Jim's desk. "Go to Q-It and type in Zach Tanner interview with Hunter Jones."

"What is the Imperial Majesty going to see if he does that?"

Andy stood, strode to the door, closed and locked it.

"Now you're scaring me, Andy."

He returned to his chair. "It had better scare you. This could be the end of our long and successful run at Q-It and the beginning of somebody's vacation in Leavenworth, or maybe the Alcatraz of the Rockies."

"Let's cut to the chase. What does this Hunter Jones have to say about Q-It?"

"Jones claimed that our search engines return biased query results."

"A lot of people have said that. We've stood up to them and refuted every legal challenge. What makes this guy any different?"

"Jones says he has proof, scientific evidence that our query results are politically biased, by design, and that we support our preferred politics and politicians."

"Andy, he—"

"That's not all. Jones says that with the U.S. polarized, fifty-fifty, Q-It controls the next presidential election."

It wasn't good, but neither was it disastrous. "Look, this Hunter Jones can insinuate whatever he wants, but it won't stand up to any legal challenge. Besides, how many people heard this mad dog foaming at the mouth?"

"Jim, it went out to a national radio network from, of all places, Medford, Oregon. A local DJ, Zach Tanner, who's a political conservative, interviewed this data-analysis guru. The network carried it, and now it's going viral on YouTube. Did you know that about thirty percent of the national news shown on TV comes from—"

"I know, I know. It comes from the Internet—the social media, other big web sites, anywhere the idiots can find their drivel."

"Regardless, it will make it back to the TV news networks. The one thing that might save us is that when Jones started making accusations that might have brought lawsuits against the radio station, Tanner cut him off."

"Maybe people will ignore him as just another nutcase or conspiracy theorist."

"Not if he has proof. We are vulnerable here, Jim. We've got to—"

"Listen, I want you to find out everything you can on this Hunter Jones."

"After you heard about the interview, I thought you'd ask, so I had my people pull up everything we could find in about sixty minutes."

"Well, is he a nutcase?"

"No. He has impeccable credentials."

"What credentials?"

"An MS in computer science from Stanford with a GPA of 3.95. He completed a certificate for the Advanced Computing Security Program at the university. Then he got an MS in Statistics-Data Science. He has precisely the credentials to do this analysis. He is writing up a research report on his findings. We can guess part of what he might say, but we don't have the data he used. And we don't know what the distribution will be for that report."

"We've got to put a cork this loose cannon. And we need to know what he knows. I want a complete briefing tomorrow at 11:00 a.m. on our prioritization rules for searching and for data presentation, including what we find but don't present to our users. Get Ravi's people involved. You can have one of his analysts do the presentation if you prefer. But I want to know exactly what this Hunter Jones thinks he has discovered. And find out who's funding his research. If it's the government, query the NTIS document database and see what else Jones has published. And check the relevant scientific journals for papers published. Also, see if you can determine how he's getting his data about our queries. If he's generating queries himself, I want the IP addresses of the computers he's using."

"Right. Then we can look on our servers, see the queries he's running, and get the query results he's using for his report. But you want all of this by 11:00 a.m. tomorrow?"

"Andy, do you want tomorrow to be a pleasant day?"

Andy's sigh blasted out his frustration. "I'll have to tell Ravi to call in some of his people. We may have to pull an overnighter."

"Fine, if that's what it takes. And, Andy?"

"You mean there's more?"

"Of course, there's more. Find out if this Hunter Jones has any skeletons in his closet or other vulnerabilities that we can use if we need to dissuade him from continuing his research. You know, things like—"

"Jim, I already checked this guy out for porn, secret embarrassing relationships, anything illegal. He's pure as the driven snow. But he recently became the guardian of an eight-year-old girl. That sounded kind of strange, so I poked around a little and found that he was given custody of the girl in the will of one of his cousins. It sounds like he's Mr. Clean—so clean that a dying mother would want this twenty-six-year-old, single man to raise her daughter."

"That's it!"

"What's it?"

"Andy, if Mr. Jones is as strait-laced as it sounds, we can get to him in one of two ways. First, we can plant data on our servers showing he visits rather unsavory, and perhaps illegal, sites on the Internet."

"You mean set him up for blackmail?"

"That's a rather *unsavory* term, don't you think?"

"Isn't that what you meant?"

"Yes, but that approach is never a sure thing. Too much can go wrong."

"We could plant evidence that he's abusing the girl."

"No. Let's use the girl in another way to persuade him to cooperate."

"Do you mean kidnap the girl and the ransom is him giving us the research data and his report?"

"Kidnap is such an ugly word. If we invoke this option, we'll just give her a nice vacation until Mr. Jones becomes rational and cuts a deal with us."

"But we don't do that sort of—"

"Of course we don't. I'll tell you who to hire if we need them." Jim paused. "Andy, do I have to remind you how high the stakes are? Everything we've accomplished, all we own, it's all on the line. We must win. The data guru must lose."

Neither Andy's eyes nor his words had provided a clear picture of his thinking on this matter. Catching him after he'd thought about the situation for a few hours, and when he was tired enough to drop his guard, seemed to be the best approach. "After the eleven o'clock meeting, where we find out what Mr. Jones thinks he's discovered, you and I will have a private meeting in my office. I want you to be prepared to give me your recommendations for closing Hunter Jones' mouth by using his skeletons, real or man-made, the girl, or anything else you come up with."

Andy's sigh sounded like a deflating tire. "When we started Q-It, I thought we were just going to develop a wonderful search engine to give everybody in the world the information they're looking for."

"And that's what we do. It's just that people don't always know what they're looking for, so we help them a bit with more enlightened suggestions. Well, you've got your marching orders."

'Yeah," Andy said. "It's going to be a long night."

"One long night to prevent Mr. Jones from shutting down Q-It is a small price to pay. And, Andy, you do remember what happened with Enron? If the courts find guilt, they punish white-collar crime worse than violent crime. All the officers of the company get orange suits, including you. So I suggest you get busy and find the best way to resolve completely the issue of Mr. Hunter Jones."

Chapter 3

AJ Scott, like most twenty-four-year-old graduate students, had a lot in common with church mice. She had worked evenings helping students online through a tutoring agency, but her income seldom covered her college and living expenses, until she became a barista.

When tuition was due, AJ frequently fell behind on her apartment rent. She had always caught up quickly, and she had enough money in her hand to do that right now.

She left through the kitchen door of her apartment, crossed the alley, and took the concrete walkway through the exquisitely manicured lawn to Mr. Jackson's door.

AJ knocked and waited.

The door swung open and the sixty-something retired military sergeant looked down at her, then his eyes refocused on the wad of cash in her hand.

"I've come to catch up on my rent, Mr. Jackson. And I'd like to extend my lease until the end of summer. That's when I graduate."

He stretched out his hand.

AJ smoothed out the bills and summed up her rent as she placed the bills one-at-a-time in his big, meaty hand. "Six-hundred and seventy-five dollars. Now, about the lease extension, I—"

"There's not going to be any extension. Since you haven't contacted me about it, I already rented the apartment. Your lease is up day after tomorrow, so you need to be completely out by tomorrow."

"But I have a good job now. I can pay."

20

"So does the man I've already rented it to."

"But there are laws. You can't just—"

"Oh, I can. In fact, I just did. Sue me if you don't like it, but you signed the lease and I'm covered by the disclaimer in it, which is approved by the state and which you probably didn't bother to read."

AJ glared at Mr. Jackson and started to call him one of several words that came to mind, but she tried to keep those words from her vocabulary.

She could fight the Grinch in court, and she might prevail. But Alicia Josephine Scott didn't go anywhere she wasn't wanted, and her landlord had made it clear he didn't want her.

But where was AJ actually wanted? The truth was no one had wanted her since her father was killed, leaving her an orphan. Certainly not the foster parents who said they wanted to adopt her. They only wanted to adopt AJ until a better job came open for Mr. Sanders. They returned her to child services, and the Sanders moved to Fort Worth. That's when the foster cycle began. AJ was cycled and recycled for seven miserable, lonely years. Then it was off to college, almost heaven by comparison.

She needed to start packing her scant belongings so she could leave tomorrow. AJ had some money and a good job, just not enough cash, at the moment, to pay first and last month's rent for a new apartment in a location where she was willing to live.

Mrs. Robbins, a widow at church, had a room she rented to college students, and she'd offered it to AJ a few weeks ago. Now she wished she had taken Mrs. Robbins up on the offer.

AJ walked back to her room and looked up the widow's number in the church directory. She entered it on her cell.

"Mrs. Robbins, this is AJ Scott. How are you today?"

"Oh, AJ, I bet you're calling about my room."

"I am. Is it—is it still available?"

"It will be in three weeks."

If she could make it for three weeks, she would have a place to stay until she found her first teaching position. "Great. I'll take it."

"That's wonderful. Stop by in a couple of weeks. I'll need your first month's rent to hold it, and then you can rent month-to-month until you find that teaching position."

"Thanks, Mrs. Robbins. I'll see you in two weeks ... well, I'll see you at church this Sunday too. Have a nice day."

AJ had just enough time this evening to pack up most of her things. She could finish packing in the morning, throw everything into the back of her SUV, and then leave for work tomorrow ... homeless.

Thankfully, the good money AJ now made working at Veneto's Espresso had given her enough for living expenses, rent, and final school expenses. She had enough available cash left that, worst case, she could find a motel room to stay in for two or three days until she decided what to do for the remainder of those three weeks.

With a good job, AJ wasn't worried. She would work something out. She always did.

***

At 10:30 a.m. AJ carried the last box out to her old Jeep SUV. She went back in and made a final check then locked the key inside and walked away.

AJ had been placed in homes that didn't feel like home while in foster care, but this was a new feeling to her, an unsettling feeling. She might not have had a real home in the past thirteen years, but AJ always had a roof over her head.

God had been good for His word about meeting her physical needs. She had questions for Him about some of the other needs, but so far, He hadn't answered those questions.

She drove away and caught Biddle Road in the edge of Central Point and turned right toward Medford.

A few minutes later, she passed under Crater Lake Highway. Only two more blocks to Veneto's Espresso, the best job and the best coffee she'd ever had.

Who would've believed she could make almost four thousand dollars per month as a barista? But Kathy was making a killing at this location and was willing to split it generously with AJ. If people only knew the markup on espresso drinks, they would probably rebel. And Kathy was far cheaper than the franchise shops.

This job had allowed AJ, over the past six weeks, to catch up on her rent and pay for the two remaining classes to complete her course requirements for an M.A. in Education at Southern Oregon University.

When AJ reached the driveway for Veneto's, named after the locally roasted beans they used, she couldn't pull into the drive-through lane.

Kathy had leased the lot of an old service station to use for her espresso drive-through. But orange cones blocked the driveway to Veneto's, and there were no lights on inside the shop.

Did Kathy have to leave unexpectedly, maybe some emergency? If so, why hadn't she called? And why the orange cones? Maybe there had been an accident.

AJ stopped, moved two of the cones and pulled in. She got out and walked to the window. There was a note taped to the inside of it.

She shielded the sun with her hand so she could read the note.

AJ,

Call me.

Kathy

So what was happening?

A knot formed in her gut as another stabilizing force in her life felt threatened. Was her godsend being sent where all good things in the life of AJ Scott went ... *away*?

AJ pulled out her cell and hit Kathy's speed dial number.

"AJ, did you see my note?"

"Yes, but what's happening? Why are we closed and surrounded by orange dunce caps?"

"Because some dunces in the county government shut us down. They came around early this morning and rolled one of those wheels on a stick around our drive-through. Then they said we can't have an espresso drive-through here, because we can only hold nine cars in the lane and the law says we must hold ten cars without leaving anyone on the street."

The knot in AJ's stomach tightened. "You mean they just shut us down?"

"That's what they did. No warning. Nothing. They just put me out of business. I don't know what I'm going to do about my lease."

AJ had some choice words for the county business bullies, but they weren't around to hear them. And the coffee chain store down the street was probably cheering because Veneto's was becoming the hottest coffee drive-through in Medford. The chain would probably get all of her business. "What are you going to do?"

"Look for another place. But good locations are hard to find. I'll have to shut down indefinitely. It's not much consolation, but you're the best barista I've ever known. I was fortunate to find you. I'll give you a good recommendation anywhere you apply. I'll mail your last check, unless you want to come by to pick it up."

"Thanks, Kathy. I'll stop by to pick it up. I'm in between apartments right now. I hope you find a good location. When you do, please give me a call."

Starbucks and Dutch Brothers paid well, but no one could equal the deal Kathy had cut her at Veneto's Espresso.

What about the deal God had just cut AJ? Jobless, homeless. She shouldn't put that on God. It sounded more like something Satan would do. Regardless, it left AJ in a car she owned, with all her worldly goods inside, and it left her in that state of being she had come to dread, to fear, and to loathe, *alone*.

Chapter 4

At 11:35 a.m., Jim Bratkowski motioned Andy into his office then closed the door.

Jim sat in his office chair.

Andy took the chair across the desk from Jim. "You know, maybe we shouldn't have done that. I never realized it until Ravi showed us the stats."

This is not where Jim wanted their conversation to go. "Shouldn't have done what?"

"You heard the numbers. In our query results, we squelch ninety percent of the news about anyone who leans to the right politically. What we do give is mostly negative and is provided by left-leaning news sources. Come on, Jim, it doesn't take a genius to figure this out."

"I hear you, Andy. A real genius, like this Hunter Jones, could not only hurt our business but also our cause of transforming and globalizing this backward, selfish nation."

Andy nodded. "And, if he was really clever, he might send some of us to prison, provided he had the money to fund a team of topnotch lawyers."

"Well, now that this has hit the news, we've got a problem. Everything we've worked so hard for could be lost due to one nosey whistleblower who has the skills to point out a dozen ways we're winning friends and influencing people. And the clock is ticking down to the explosion, the release of that research report."

"You're the CEO. What are we going to do about it?"

"This the kind of problem one can either buy off or pry off."

"I prefer the sound of buy off. But how much is our CEO willing to spend?"

"There is the possibility that Mr. Jones can't be bought for any price."

Jim detected significant resistance in Andy to the course of action they would probably have to take. That might force him to make Andy an offer he couldn't refuse or, perhaps, give him a job that kept him in check.

"We'll have to quietly contact this Hunter Jones and feel him out on—let's put it this way. We'll offer him a publishing contract, where we get exclusive rights to his research report for a fair price."

Andy's forehead wrinkled as his eyebrows rose. "Exclusive rights? Buying him out could be expensive. Where will we get this money?"

Jim drummed his fingers on his desk. Looking like he was weighing options might conceal the fact that he'd already made up his mind. It might cause Andy to drop his guard a bit. "There's money left in the R&D budget for the cancelled cloud load-balancing project. If I remember correctly, we have about two million dollars. I've heard it said that if a person were to take one and a half million dollars and invest wisely in stocks and bonds, they would never have to work another day of their life. We'll run that by Mr. Hunter Jones and see if he takes the bait."

"Suppose he doesn't?'

"Then we pry him off by threatening legal action."

"And if that fails?"

"Maybe we'll give him a stronger incentive. We can hire someone to intimidate Mr. Hunter personally, perhaps through the girl in his custody."

"What if they trace things back to us?"

"Our job, Andy, is to make sure that they can't."

"Suppose Mr. Jones won't bend and won't quit?

"I really don't want to go there. But if worse comes to worst we have to—"

The door opened and a head poked into the room. "Sorry to disturb you, sir. But you said to let you know immediately if Hunter Jones appeared to be up to something."

"It's okay, Ken," Jim said. "What have you got?"

"We just saw Jones online, looking for two plane tickets."

"So he's taking a trip with his little charge. Where's he going?"

"He bought two tickets in first class to Washington DC, Reagan National Airport."

Not good. "When does this happen, Ken?"

"Day after tomorrow."

"Thanks. Let us know if his plans change."

"Will do, Mr. B."

Ken backed out of the room and closed the door.

Andy shook his head. "After what Jones just disclosed on national radio and on YouTube, we have to expect the worst. He could be going to Congress to the Judiciary Committee or—"

"Or the president, if that clown is willing to talk to him. We've got to stop Jones. We can't allow him to talk to anyone in DC about potential research findings on our search engines. If this guy's good enough, he could expose everything, destroy everything."

"So what do we do?"

"You mean what do *you* do, Andy?"

Andy straightened in his chair. "I'm not going to be the fall guy."

"That's a pessimistic way of looking at things. You do this job right and you could be setting yourself up to inherit my position when I retire."

Andy's frown faded. "What do I have to do?"

28

"It's really rather simple. You hire someone from that black operations outfit to—"

"To murder him?"

"That's a crude way of putting it. I would say something more like making queries for Hunter Jones return nothing."

"Don't you mean return an obituary?"

"Look, our board members don't have to know any details of our decision, only that you wanted to stop Mr. Jones from publishing his report, and I agreed in principle. And you *will* back me on this decision."

"So now you're telling me?"

Jim nodded, dipping his head deeply.

"This is getting out of hand and you're scaring me, Jim."

"Good. Then we have a mutual understanding. And I've got a brilliant idea. You're going to make a phone call, and I'm going to listen to it." Andy hadn't had the guts to go to any authorities and report this before the fact. And now that he was in on the planning, and would make the phone call, he was more than just an accessory. That should eliminate any thoughts about reporting this after the fact.

Andy's eyes widened. "So you're going to hire the Captain to kill Hunter Jones?"

"No. You're going to hire the Captain to abduct Hunter's little girl for ransom, the ransom being the research findings and the report. Killing Hunter Jones only becomes necessary if the ransom approach fails. We need to move on this today, and the job has to be complete before Jones climbs on that plane day after tomorrow. And you, Andy, get to be the Captain's supervisor. Here's his number. Pull out your cell and call him."

Andy's protruding Adam's apple bobbed as he swallowed hard.

Chapter 5

So this is what it feels like to be homeless.

AJ hadn't a clue where she would spend the next three weeks while she waited for her room to become available. Nor did she know where she would spend this night.

What she needed was some quiet time to sort out the unsettling questions assaulting her mind. Besides, God would make a way for her, wouldn't He?

Wish, worry, and pray. With Jesus in their lives, Christians were supposed to be able to live above that. But it's what her life had been filled with lately, and there was a great place to pray about her worry about fifteen miles out Crater Lake Highway.

AJ pulled out of Veneto's Espresso with all her worldly goods stuffed into the back of her old SUV. She had to leave behind the few pieces of furniture she'd acquired from several trips to Goodwill. But better times lay ahead of her. Maybe she could buy something worth keeping next time.

She took the ramp to northbound Crater Lake Highway. From here, her old Jeep Cherokee could almost drive itself to the little out-of-the-way park she'd discovered last summer.

On this warm, sunny June morning, the quiet park along the Rogue River would be deserted. She could sit in the grass by the river and try to decide how to spend the next few nights without exhausting what little cash remained after paying the tuition for her final classes and for her master's exam. Then she could begin her search for a teaching position.

If she ran out of time, she could always spend tonight in her SUV. Maybe in a rest area along I-5.

At this time of year, a cheap but decent motel room, one without bed bugs or drunks roaming the halls, would cost eighty to one-hundred dollars per night. AJ had almost three-hundred dollars in her purse, another thousand in her checking account, thanks to the generous wages Kathy had paid her. But her charge card was nearly maxed out.

Alone, homeless, and her life careening out of control. That was AJ Scott.

With so much seemingly out of control, she needed to be in control of something.

Music had been a light that had brought her through many a dark moment in her life. She pulled a loose CD from the storage space under the stereo console and shoved it in the player.

In a few seconds the CD errored off. The stereo ejected the CD and went to radio mode. The radio was tuned in to a local news station where a news commentator reported that a woman had been attacked while sleeping in her car at a rest area on I-5 near Grants Pass.

So much for sleeping in her car at a rest area.

AJ shoved the CD in again.

After about thirty seconds, she got the same result from her slowly dying stereo system. Except the news was over, and the radio station was playing music.

But music on the radio, played at the whims of some DJ, would be one more thing out of her control, one too many.

She turned off the stereo.

It was silent in the car except for the hum of tires on pavement. And that left AJ where she had been for far too long ... alone.

And why was she always alone? This question raised another, the one she could never answer.

Could anyone made in God's image be unlovable?
Could anyone be so badly broken that no one would love
them?

A few minutes later, she turned off the highway onto Rogue River Drive. A hundred yards up the drive, AJ turned into the park and rolled down a long, tree-lined parking area that extended almost to the river.

She chose a parking spot nearer the street and decided to walk down to the boat ramp and find a grassy spot to sit by the river. AJ slid out of her seat and stood beside her Jeep.

A young couple's laughter rose above the soft rush of the river. It came from the building tucked into the trees on the edge of the park.

The building, called The River House, was a popular wedding venue and that appeared to be what the young couple, now in each other's arms, had in mind.

A wedding, a family, people who loved her—maybe they weren't in the cards for AJ. But she walked back toward the street to get a better view of The River House and the couple enjoying themselves.

The young man and woman walked away from the building toward their car, apparently leaving.

The sounds of shoes pounding the pavement came from across Rogue River Drive.

AJ turned toward the rhythmic noises.

Two figures flew across a public parking area, crossed the road, and entered the park. The tall person was almost dragging the short person, a girl about eight or nine. The man frequently looked back, as if someone were chasing them.

A row of short trees hid AJ from their view.

But what was she witnessing? A kidnapping?

She hurried back to her Jeep. Maybe she should climb back in and leave like the young couple at The River House had done.

AJ slid in, locked her car doors, and put the key in the ignition, ready for a quick get-away.

The two runners passed about forty feet behind her car. They didn't appear to have seen her through the SUV's tinted glass windows. When the two approached the boat ramp, they turned toward the thick bushes and trees lining the river.

AJ scanned the street and parking area the man and girl had ran across, but she saw no one pursuing them.

She looked back toward the river.

The man emerged from the bushes, but he was alone.

A shiver spread through shoulders. Had the man done something to the girl? Had she just witnessed a murder? Well, sort of witnessed it?

The man cut diagonally across the park and hit Rogue River Drive sprinting at an incredible rate. He looked like someone the U.S. Olympic Track Team should recruit. But was he running away from a crime he'd committed or from criminals chasing him?

Instead of heading back toward town, the man ran away from it, toward the hills and forested land to the west, where a few scattered houses populated the hillsides.

AJ got out of her car and moved to a spot where an opening in the trees gave her a view down Rogue River Drive.

The man had nearly run out of sight, when the sounds of more shoes slapping the pavement came from across Rogue River Drive.

Two men in gray sweats and running shoes sprinted from a paved parking area out onto the street. They stopped and scanned the roadway until their gazes locked on the lone runner.

The two spotted him just before he rounded a bend. They pursued him, running hard but not as fast as the running machine who had sprinted past AJ in the park.

From her vantage point, AJ could see the lone runner veer off the drive and onto Sawyer Road. Now trees blocked her view.

Maybe he was heading for the forest that lined a creek bed that ran up this side of the mountain.

He probably intended to lose them in the trees. With the steep climb and his running ability, he could run away from the two men.

A short distance down the street, one of the gray-clad runners pulled something from under his sweatshirt.

AJ drew a sharp breath.

A gun.

This painted the man and the girl in something closer to white. The gunmen were the bad guys. The man must have hidden the girl so he could outrun their pursuers.

But could she be sure?

And what about the girl ... or her dead body?

You need to leave, now!

But maybe I can rescue the girl from who knows what?

This isn't safe. You need to go.

She choked the nagging voice into silence.

AJ had to check to see what happened to the girl. But dread about what she might find sent her heart into a wild percussion solo. It beat against her sternum while scenes from horror movies she should never have watched played through her mind.

AJ trotted to the boat ramp, then she looked to her left into the bushes lining the river.

No movement.

She stopped and listened.

Above the rush of the river, almost blending with it, came soft pulsating sounds. Maybe someone crying.

Dead bodies don't cry.

If the man had hidden the girl, she was in danger.

AJ stepped toward the bushes, then stopped. How would the girl react to a stranger approaching her?

And what if the gunmen returned?

Whatever AJ was going to do, she needed to do quickly. And she needed to become invisible to anyone approaching.

She pushed some branches aside, stepped between bushes and out of sight of anyone in the park.

When she looked across a small opening in the vegetation, AJ froze.

Chapter 6

As he sprinted up Rogue River Drive, Hunter glanced behind him. Still no one in sight.

He replayed the words he had roared out at Sam two minutes ago.

"Stay here, Sam. Don't move."

"Please don't leave me. I want to go with you."

"It's too dangerous. I'm going to lose those guys and come back for you."

"Hunter, I—"

"No. Stay where you are! You move and I'll kill you, Sam! I mean it."

Hunter had completely lost it when he roared at Sam. But her life was at stake. If she didn't stay hidden, the men would find her.

If Hunter was right about why he was being chased, the men were desperate enough even to kill a young girl. Scaring her was the only thing he could think of at the time.

He would have to win Sam's trust again when he came back for her, but Sam would be alive.

Hunter had made the right choice.

He looked back before he rounded a turn and lost sight of the entrance to the park.

The two men who had chased Sam and Hunter ran out of the park and onto Rogue River Drive. One pointed at Hunter. They sprinted toward him.

He swerved to the side of the road, cutting off their view of him. Hopefully, the two men hadn't seen him long enough to realize Sam wasn't with him.

Hunter veered onto Sawyer Road. In another hundred yards he would cut straight up the hill into the dense trees.

At least the two men were following *him*, not looking for Sam. And Hunter would bet his life that he could outrun them going up this mountain.

In reality, he had just bet Sam's life, because if they couldn't catch him, they would eventually realize Sam couldn't maintain this brutal pace.

That's when they would go back to the park and begin a search for the person Hunter loved more than any other on this fallen planet, Samantha Wilson, the girl they could use to manipulate Hunter.

If he ran a large semi-circular pattern on the mountainside, he could double back and beat the pursuers to Sam. If he and Sam could reach his car without being seen, Hunter would take her away, however far he needed to keep her safe.

For now, running through the forest would become the proverbial cat and mouse game. But when would the men give up the chase and double back?

That Hunter couldn't predict, so ...

Let the game begin.

***

A loud crack sounded when a dry branch broke under the weight of AJ's one-hundred and twenty-five pounds.

A young girl's head jerked around. Her face held wide, questioning eyes. Tear tracks streaked her cheeks.

"Are you one of them?" Her voice was ragged like a child who had cried far too long.

The impulse to run to the girl, scoop her up, and hold her shot through AJ's heart. The impulse demanded action. Protect her. Console her. AJ had to do something.

AJ stuffed her emotions and chose her words carefully. "Do you mean the men in the gray sweats?"

The girl nodded slowly as her eyes scanned AJ from head to foot. Those eyes locked on AJ's face.

"I'm not one of them. They're—"

"They're bad men. They have guns, and I think they want to kill Hunter."

"Hunter? You mean your dad?"

"No. My mom and dad are dead." The girl's beautiful face contorted into a tortured caricature of itself.

AJ took a step toward the girl.

She shrank away until her back bumped into a tree trunk.

"I'm not going to hurt you."

"Then maybe you should just go away."

"I want to help you, because ..."

The girl's eyes blinked and softened. She had dropped her guard a little. "Because of what? And how do I know you're not one of *them*?"

"Because I'm too much like *you* to be one of *them*."

The girl rose from her knees to a crouching position. Golden locks of curly hair fell from her shoulders. A frown creased her tanned forehead. "What do you mean by *like me*?"

"My mom and dad died when I was about your age, but I didn't—who is Hunter?"

"He's my guardian. I call him uncle but he's really my cousin." The girl stood.

She was about four and a half feet tall, thin, but she moved like an athlete, not like most little girls. She just wasn't a tall enough athlete to keep up with Hunter the runner.

"What's your name?"

"Why should I tell you?" The girl balled her fists and gave AJ a defiant glare.

"Because I know exactly how you feel, aching inside for someone to love you, missing those who did, and wondering if life will ever be good again."

The glare vanished. Tears welled and overflowed onto her cheeks.

AJ extended her arms and the young girl ran into them.

AJ held her as she cried.

But the girl wasn't crying alone.

In only a few seconds, the bond had been forged, connecting one orphan's life to another's in a way that people who have never been truly alone in this world could never understand.

"I'm Sam," the girl said in a hoarse whisper.

She met Sam's gaze and studied the girl's eyes for a moment. "I want you to know this, Sam. When I help someone, I don't quit. I'm in this to the end, until you're safe. I mean that."

AJ kissed Sam's forehead.

"Thanks. But what—"

"Come on, Sam, we need to see what's happening out by the street. We wouldn't want them sneaking up on us."

"But how will Hunter find me if we leave? He told me to stay here."

"Does he have a cell phone?"

"Yeah."

"Did he have it with him?"

"Yeah."

"And you know his number?"

Sam nodded.

"Then I'll call him and tell him where we are."

"Then I guess it's okay." Sam gave AJ her hand.

AJ led her out of the heavy vegetation, making sure they left on the opposite side from where they had entered.

"This will take us around the house." AJ pointed to the right of a small outbuilding toward a deck under some large trees.

"There are paved walkways and a deck we can walk on. Much quieter than walking in dry leaves and brush. And we can watch the park through the trees to see who comes looking for you, those two gunmen or Hunter?"

Chapter 7

AJ studied Sam as the girl walked beside her. Who could possibly want to harm an angel like her?

Sam looked up at her. "Hunter said those men might want me too."

AJ had hoped that wasn't the case. "Did he tell you why?"

"He didn't know for sure. Maybe it was something to do with his research. Hunter was in the news this week. On the radio, TV, the Internet, and in some newspapers. Didn't you see him?"

So Hunter was some kind of celebrity. "No. I've been a bit preoccupied with my own problems for the last few days."

AJ led Sam on a walkway that circled part of the house. Soon they came to a covered deck. It looked like it was made for wedding ceremonies. A little farther and they could look through the trees into the park.

When they reached a secluded vantage point for watching the park, AJ stopped. "This spot will work."

Sam shook her head. "Not if someone comes around the house the same way we did."

"You're pretty smart for a ... uh ..."

"A nine-year-old," Sam finished for her. "Well, almost nine."

The park was vacant and there were no signs of runners on the street. AJ focused on Sam. What must life be like for her? "What's it like living with your cousin, is it?"

"My friends at school say they think it would be awful. But if I can't have Mom and Dad, Hunter would be my first choice."

"Your first choice. Why is that, Sam?"

"He tries so hard to be both a mom and a dad to me. Sometimes he tries too hard. But I don't make it easy for him. I drive him crazy, but I don't mean to. I can't help it. I'm a handful."

"I can see that." AJ sensed a smile curling the corners of her mouth. Her first smile in hours.

Sam looked up at her. "What should I call you?"

"I guess I didn't introduce myself properly."

"No. You scared me then ..." Tears welled once again in Sam's bright blue eyes.

"Yes, then." AJ laid a hand on Sam's shoulder. "I'm going to tell you a secret if you promise to tell no one, ever. Promise?"

Sam's head dipped as she watched AJ warily.

"Promise you won't laugh?"

"I promise."

"My name is Alicia Josephine Scott."

"That's—" Sam's hand slapped over her mouth and her shoulders shook.

"Sam, you promised."

"But that's eight or nine syllabuses long."

"You mean syllables?"

"Whatever. But if I needed help, I might die before I could call you. I hope I don't have to call you that."

"I said it was a secret. Nobody calls me Alicia Josephine."

"What do they call you?"

"AJ. Sometimes people I work with call me Scotty."

"Scotty sounds like a boy's name. I'm gonna call you AJ."

The sounds of shoes on pavement reached them.

Movement flashed through the trees on her right.

A runner from the street slowed and jogged into the park.

Sam's eyes widened.

"It'll be okay, Sam. Just keep still and keep quiet until we check this out." AJ pulled Sam down behind a bush that hid them but gave them a view of the upper end of the park.

The runner wore gray sweats.

Sam looked up at AJ and mouthed the words, "That's one of them."

AJ nodded and then watched the man as he slowed to a walk. He seemed to be scanning the trees on both sides of the parking lot as he walked away from them and toward the river.

He had to be looking for Sam. What would he do when he reached the boat ramp at the river?

Sam raised up and put her mouth by AJ's ear. "What if they find where I was and then come here looking for me?"

AJ lowered her voice. "They don't know about me. I'll be a big surprise to them."

"But what will you do?"

"I'm still working on that." AJ leaned forward to watch the man's progress down the park. She stood and leaned forward to see what he was doing near the boat ramp.

She lost her balance and nearly fell forward into the open where she might have exposed herself.

Sam's hand touched the back of AJ's neck. Her tank top nearly choked her as Sam tugged hard, trying to keep AJ from falling.

After she regained her balance, AJ turned, cupped Sam's cheek, and mouthed, "Thanks."

When she turned to see the man, he had pulled out his gun and appeared to be studying the spot where Sam and AJ had entered the bushes.

He stopped, examined some foliage, then brought his gun to firing position and crept into the spot where Hunter had hidden Sam.

Sam smoothed AJ's tank top where she had yanked on it. "When he sees where I was, he's gonna come looking around The River House, isn't he?"

"He might. Follow me, Sam, and walk softly."

"And carry a big stick?"

"Where'd you hear that?"

"Hunter says it a lot. It means you don't have to act like a bully, but you gotta be ready to fight."

"And that's what I'm going to do. Now let's walk around that house and I'll look for one."

Sam's forehead wrinkled. "For a bully or a fight?"

"Neither. For a big stick."

When AJ and Sam approached the raised deck, AJ spotted a pipe set into the ground in an open area. It looked like something intended to hold a large umbrella.

She grabbed the pipe and twisted.

It turned.

She pulled and it slid out of its hole.

The heavy metal pipe was longer than her arm, a couple of inches in diameter, and it weighed about five pounds.

When she gripped it with both hands, other than being a bit heavier, it had the feel of the handle of a baseball bat. "Move to the corner of the house, but stay behind me, Sam."

"If he comes up here, are you gonna hit him like a baseball?"

"That's the idea." It wouldn't be the first time she'd clobbered someone with a bat, but that was a different world and a different AJ. This wouldn't be done out of anger, but self-defense and mostly for Sam.

"If he comes this way, won't you have to swing it backwards?"

"I'm a southpaw, Sam."

Sam's forehead wrinkled. "A paw from the south? A polar bear from the South Pole?"

"No. I'm a left hander. That's what they call us in baseball."

"So you played baseball?" Sam's whisper blasted out a little too loudly.

"Women's fastpitch softball."

"Could you hit home runs?"

"Yes. Now you need to be quiet. I hear something."

Soft sounds of footsteps came from around the corner of the house. Then the thumping of shoes on wood.

The gunman had almost reached the corner.

AJ reached back and pushed Sam's head downward.

Sam got the idea. She was to stay back and stay down.

AJ took her batting stance, hands barely hidden by the corner of the house. She waited for the pitch.

The ball arrived high and a bit outside.

AJ swung for the fence.

The barrel of the improvised bat sounded a loud tink, like a magnesium bat, when it caught the oversized ball above the right eye.

The gray-clad man fell backward and dropped hard onto the deck. It was a home run. Maybe a grand slam.

The man's gun slid across the deck and dropped onto a brick-paved path.

"Grand salami. Break out the rye bread, Sam. But don't look at the guy."

"I'm not hungry. Besides I want to see what you did to— oh, gross." Sam ran to the edge of the deck and puked.

AJ leaped off the deck and grabbed the man's gun.

He still lay motionless.

Sam wretched a second time then slowly turned toward AJ. Sam wiped her mouth then pointed at the man. "Did you kill him?"

"I doubt it. It's not as bad as it looks. Even a slight head wound can leave a lot of blood."

The only movement was the victim's rib cage, moving in and out with each breath. He was out cold or maybe worse.

"So you really did play baseball or something?"

"Or something. Now let's get out of here before he wakes up or his partner comes looking for him." She took Sam's hand and tugged. "The white SUV across the parking area is mine. Hurry, Sam."

They scurried through trees and across the narrow parking area to AJ's old SUV.

Sam wrinkled her nose. "Does it run?"

"Most of the time. Get in. It's not as bad as it looks."

Sam opened her door and leaned in. "What's all that stuff in the back?"

"Everything I own."

Sam's eyes widened. "Please tell me I'm not being kidnapped by a homeless lady who lives in her car?"

"You're not being kidnapped, and I don't live in my car."

Sam slid in. "But you are homeless, aren't you?"

"You need to buckle in, Sam. And whether I'm homeless or not, we need to get out of here."

They both fastened their seatbelts.

AJ dropped the gun on the console and hit the ignition.

The engine turned but didn't start.

"Darn!"

"Most of the time?" Sam said. "This must be the rest of the time."

"Oh, ye of little faith." AJ hit the starter and the engine fired. "Watch for the other gunman or Hunter while I get us out of here."

The wheels squealed as AJ spun a quick U-turn and drove toward the street. She turned right onto Rogue River Drive headed back to Crater Lake Highway.

Sam's small hand clutched AJ's shoulder. "A man just ran down the road behind us. He's watching us."

Great! Now they would see which way she turned.

Which way would that be? Left or right? Toward Medford or Crater Lake and Eastern Oregon?

AJ hadn't a clue which was safest.

"Eeny, meeny, miny, moe!"

"I thought you knew what you were *doing*." Sam's voice crescendoed on her last word.

"Moe is right, but it doesn't feel right." AJ yanked the wheel to the left and pressed the accelerator to the floor.

"AJ, that man was staring at us. He saw us turn."

Chapter 8

It was half past noon, almost an hour since Hunter left Sam. As much as he wanted to run pell-mell into the park and scoop her up in his arms, the situation called for caution. And he first needed to descend the hill into the edge of town to complete his big semi-circle run on the mountain that would bring him back to the park and to Sam.

Hunter relaxed and coasted down the mountainside. His long stride carried him over patches of poison oak that dotted the hillside above Shady Cove.

What was it his botanist friend had said? The most populous plant in Jackson County, not counting the grasses, was poison oak. Good thing Hunter had acquired immunity after being covered with its itchy rash as a kid.

At the base of the mountain, Hunter the hit the street that would take him to Rogue River Drive near the entrance to the park.

When he last saw one of the gunmen, the man was trying to track Hunter through the trees above Sawyer Road. No way could he have beaten Hunter back to the park. But what about the other gunman? He could be in the park looking for Sam.

Hunter stopped a few yards from Rogue River Drive. He scanned the park.

Nothing moving in the park. But, to be safe, he would walk around The River House without exposing himself to anyone in the park. He needed to go now before the gunmen showed up.

Hunter exploded out of his stance like a runner coming out of the starting blocks. He sprinted across the street and through the parking lot to the house and stopped between The River House and the trees shielding him from the park.

A noise that didn't belong to this setting sounded above the rush of the Rogue River and the birds chirping. It sounded like someone groaning, someone on the other side of the house.

Hunter crept to the house and followed its perimeter which took him toward the deck on the far side. When he reached the corner, he peered around it.

A body lay partly on the deck, head and shoulders drooping off the deck by wooden steps.

He looked more closely.

Hands pressed against a bloody head as if the man was trying to hold his head together. He wore gray sweats.

It was the second gunman. But what had happened to him?

As clever and strong as she was for a nine-year-old, Sam could never have done this. And where was Sam? The place he had hidden her was only fifty yards away, in bushes near the river.

Hunter sprinted the walkway behind the house and slid to a stop beside the tangle of bushes where he had left Sam.

He pushed some branches aside and stuck his head in. "Sam?"

No answer.

His heart accelerated into a driving rhythm that threatened to beat itself to death against his sternum.

Sam was gone.

It was too coincidental that a man who had been looking for Hunter and Sam, intending violence, had found it hardly fifty yards from where Sam sat hidden.

Maybe the man with the bashed in the head was conscious. He might know where they had taken Sam. She wouldn't have moved of her own free will. His ferocious words would have prevented that.

Hunter ran back to the deck and slowed as he approached the body of the man.

A dark crimson puddle of blood flooded the wooden step below the man's head. He groaned and then slid his upper body onto the deck without raising his bloodied head.

Most of the bleeding had stopped, leaving his face smeared with partly dried blood. It came from the wide, oozing cut above his right eyebrow. The cut could use a few stitches.

Weapons. Where was the guy's gun? Hunter patted the man's pockets. Nothing there. But a three-foot section of steel pipe lay on the ground on the far side of the deck. Hunter stepped off the deck and picked it up.

Traces of blood dotted one end of the pipe. The steel pipe had been used to deck the guy on the deck.

Hunter gripped the pipe like a baseball bat and strode back to the injured man.

He remained stretched out on the deck moaning. But now his moans came wrapped around what sounded like words.

"Somebody, help me."

Hunter stood beside the man and held the bat like he intended to use it.

"Don't hit me again. Please."

"I didn't hit you, but I'd like to know who did. Was it a small girl?"

The man coughed and wiped his mouth, streaking his face with partly dried blood. "You got to be kidding. It was some Amazon of a woman. Big, strong. That's all I can remember before the lights went out."

"Look at me, dude. Do you know who I am?"

The man blinked twice, then his eyes widened with recognition.

"I can see that you do. Now listen closely, because I'm only going to ask once, and if I don't get the right answer, I'm going to finish the job this Amazon woman started. Are you following me, dude?"

"Yeah." The man answered with a growl.

"Where is the girl with long blond hair?"

"I—I don't know. I never saw her."

Hunter wouldn't allow anyone to play games when Sam's safety was in question.

"All right. You asked for it." He raised the pipe over his head.

"Wait! Wait! I can explain."

Hunter lowered the pipe to waist high as if lining up a chopping blow to the man's head. "Okay, explain."

"I came back to look for the girl, but I didn't find her. When I came around the house, some huge woman caught me in the face with a lucky swing."

"From the looks of you, I would say it wasn't luck. Somebody knows how to swing a bat. She's probably left-handed too, from where that gash is on your forehead and where you're lying. But what about the girl. My girl!"

"I don't know. The only thing that makes sense is that the woman took her."

"Why, dude?"

"Like I said, I don't know. You got to believe me. Is—is there a light-colored Jeep in the parking lot?"

"There's nothing in the parking lot."

"Then the woman took the girl in her car."

Hunter raised the pipe. "And like I said, why, dude?"

"Please. You've got to believe me."

The guy's partner might be arriving anytime now, and he had a gun. Hunter had seen enough to know that.

"Okay. I've got something you've got to believe, and you'd better convince your boss back at Q-It. If one hair on Sam's head is out of place, if she's frightened and traumatized, if she's hurt in anyway, I will kill you, your partner, and whoever hired you at Q-It. And tell Mr. Bratkowski that unless Sam is returned to me safe and unharmed within twelve hours, Bratkowski won't be safe in his cushy, Seattle corner office. He makes a great target for my McMillan Tactical Rifle when he's sitting behind the big glass windows of his corner office. Can you remember all that?"

The man nodded.

"Good. Shall I give you a taste of what you'll get if you forget?"

"No, dude. I've got it."

"You're not going to die on me before you deliver my message, are you?"

"No. I'm just a bit dizzy and ... this headache ..."

"After your partner finds you, you will deliver my message to your supervisor at Q-It and to Bratkowski."

Hunter lowered the pipe but decided to keep it in case he needed a weapon. He whirled and ran across the parking area of The River House and stopped at the street.

There was no one coming down Rogue River Drive, so he cut diagonally across the street and ran back toward town where he'd left his pickup.

Hunter's truck sat in the parking lot of a convenience store by the Valero station that Hunter and Sam had been chased from when the gunmen surprised them. He opened the driver's door, tossed the pipe in the passenger seat, and climbed in.

If he could find a light-colored Jeep, driven by some home-run-hitting Amazon, maybe he could find Sam. How could he start his search?

He was parked along the main drag through Shady Cove. If the Amazon lady had headed out the highway, she would have passed this store.

It was a longshot but, right now, that's all Hunter had.

Thanks to Oregon's ban on self-service gas stations, an attendant would have been near the street.

A young man in his early twenties stood one lane over, removing the nozzle from a gas tank.

Hunter approached him. "Dude, I think someone just took off with my daughter in their car. Did you see a light-colored Jeep go by here a few minutes ago?"

The attendant hung the hose on the pump and looked up. "You need to call the police if you think your daughter might have been abducted."

"I will, but I need to know which way she went."

"She, you say?"

"Yeah. A woman. A big woman with a nine-year-old girl."

"About ten minutes ago, a light gray Jeep almost hit a car right in front of the station. The Jeep slammed on its brakes, left some rubber on the street. Nobody hit anybody, but they sure scared a little old lady. All's well that ends well. Except for your daughter being taken."

Hunter's heart redlined. "Was the Jeep going out Crater Lake Highway?"

"Yes. Headed up the road toward Trail."

"Did you see the driver?"

"Sort of. I think it was a woman. Don't know how big she was, but she had a shorter passenger with her. Passed by right in front of me, on the wrong side of the street. She laid a patch of rubber and fishtailed when she tore out of here like a bat out of Hades. The old lady standing at the curb thought she was toast."

"Ten minutes ago, you say?"

"About. But you'd better call the police if she's got your girl with her. The way that woman was driving, maybe she was high or something."

Though it was almost noon, Hunter's stomach churned like it might give up whatever was left of his breakfast. "Yeah. I will. Thanks."

Great. Now it was an Amazon, high on crack or speed, driving recklessly with Sam in her car.

Hunter still had that steel pipe. And when he found the ogress, he was tempted to do to her what she had evidently done to the gunman, put a big dent in her forehead.

Chapter 9

Shortly after one o'clock, Hunter sat in his truck at the gas station in Shady Cove, waiting for a line of cars to clear so he could pull out onto Crater Lake Highway.

His cell sounded the alarm for an incoming call.

The caller ID displayed a local number, one not in his contacts list.

Was this the crackhead who had Sam?

He answered, opting for caution. "Hello."

"Is this Hunter Jones?" A woman's voice.

"Could be. Or I could be your worst nightmare."

"It's him." The voice in the background sounded like Sam.

"Is Sam okay? I want to talk to her, now."

"Sam is fine."

"I want to hear her tell me that."

"You will, in a minute. How can I trust that you're who you say you are?"

"Give Sam the phone and you'll see."

"No, not yet."

"Why?"

"I don't trust people I can't see. Most people can't be trusted, regardless. They let you down, even when they say they won't."

"If people always let people down, then why should I trust you with Sam?"

"I guess because you have no choice."

"Oh, I have a choice, all right. I may have to leave Sam in your care for the moment, but I don't have to trust you."

"Look, buster, I found Sam in the bushes where you left her alone, scared, and crying. I risked my life to get her out of there and away from those two gunmen, whoever they were."

"So you know about them?"

"I watched you when you entered the park, when you left, and when those two chased you up the road."

"Yeah. Guess you were there, if you knew about the two gunmen. I ran across one of them. He had gotten his forehead bashed in. Do you know anything about that?"

"You saw him?'

"Yeah."

"Was he ... was he alive?"

"He was. When I asked him what happened, he said some Amazon woman surprised him." Hunter paused. "Let me give you a clue, then you can tell me if I win the game or not. It's Ms. Amazon, on the deck, with the steel pipe."

"You know, if I were you, and didn't trust the person who had your girl, I wouldn't keep insulting them. Amazon. You should be more careful about calling people names."

"Well, are you one? You haven't denied it."

"Of all the—"

"It's Hunter. He doesn't mean to be a jerk. Sometimes he just can't help it." Sam's voice came from the background again.

"I want to talk to Sam, now."

"Sam, do you want to talk to this man who doesn't trust me and calls me names?"

"I'll talk to him. I can handle Hunter."

Rustling sounds came through the phone followed by Sam's short, little breaths.

"Sam, are you okay?"

"Yes. Just a little bit scared, because some people are trying to find us. But AJ protected me."

AJ. So that was the name of the Amazon crackhead. "Let me talk to AJ again."

"Here she is, but she doesn't look happy. I'd watch out if I were you, Uncle Hunter."

"I'm not your uncle, Sam."

"You *are* Sam's legal guardian, right?"

He ignored the question. "AJ. What's that stand for? Amazon Jane?"

The other end went silent.

She didn't sound like some dopehead, and she had saved Sam and performed some dangerous heroics in the process.

Worrying about Sam, things spiraling out of control, and the danger not nearly over—he had lost it, flipped out and possibly put them all in danger.

"Sorry, AJ. When I couldn't find Sam, I went a little crazy and took it out on you."

"Are you apologizing for calling me an Amazon or asking forgiveness for being who you are?"

"What's that supposed to mean?" He blew out a breath in frustration. "Forget I said that. Just tell me this, are you two safe for now?"

"We were being chased by a dark-colored SUV. I think we lost it, then I turned off the highway and hid. I've only been in the area for about eighteen months. I'm a grad student at Southern Oregon University. I don't know the roads very well. I need a good place to hide from them."

"Where are you now?"

"The road just split—a big Y in the highway. One way said Crater Lake. The other said Diamond Lake."

"Which way did you go?"

"Toward Crater Lake, but I wanted to lose them, so we turned left onto a little forest road shortly after the Y intersection."

"Did you see the number of the road?"

"It's NF-6260, I think."

He knew the location from his fishing and hunting trips in that area. "Go up the road and turn left at each intersection you come to. I think there are only a couple of turns to make. In about two miles, you'll come back to the highway, along the other fork of the Y. It's Highway 230, headed toward Diamond Lake and on to Eastern Oregon. When you get on the highway, keep your speed above the limit."

"But I don't need another speeding ticket."

"Another one? You must really like speed. How about meth?"

"I thought we had gotten beyond the name calling. But maybe jerks can't manage to do that."

"Sorry, AJ. I've kept Sam beside me almost every waking minute since her mother died. I guess I'm a little freaked out right now." He paused. "Look. If police stop you, that's a good thing. You can tell them two gunmen are chasing you and they want to—" Hunter stopped. He couldn't say kill, not with Sam involved and maybe listening. "They're trying to abduct Sam. But there probably won't be any police so, by the time those guys figure out what you did, you'll have a big head start. I'm headed your way and will try to catch up to you before they do."

"I'm sure glad somebody knows these roads."

"Hunter knows almost everything." Sam's voice again.

'Then why does he think I'm Amazon Jane?"

"I should have told you. When it comes to girls, he's clueless."

"Sam, I'm glad that you think I'm a girl and not Amazon Jane." She paused. "Hunter, I should have let you know. I've got a gun. That guy I clobbered with the pipe—I took his."

"Why does that not make me feel any better about this situation? Whatever you do, AJ, don't point it at Sam."

"I'm not exactly stupid."

"That's being debated as we speak."

"So you aren't worried I might point it at myself?"

"That's being debated too. Do you know how to handle a gun?"

"There's not much to it. You point it at something you want to be dead, and you pull the trigger."

"Give the girl a marksmanship ribbon."

"So you agree with Sam. I see that I've improved from an Amazon to a normal girl."

"I didn't say normal."

'Look, Hunter, you can trust me to do whatever I have to do to keep her safe."

"Whatever ..."

"Was that a question or a smart remark?"

"Let me talk to Sam again."

"What's the magic word?"

Sam giggled in the background. All things considered, it was a good sign.

Rustling noises and static-like sounds came as the phone changed hands.

"Whatcha' want, Hunter?"

"I want you to describe AJ to me."

Whispered words he couldn't discern came through the phone.

"Well ... she's big." Sam's voice. "Really big. She could probably hold you down and make you say uncle."

"Sam, did AJ tell you to say that?"

"Uh, AJ says you shouldn't check girls out over the phone. It's rude."

"We're getting nowhere fast. Put AJ back on."

"I'm here. What do you want now, my height, weight and my measurements?"

"Are you offering?"

"Like you said, we're getting nowhere fast. I just want to go somewhere safe and hide until you reach us. Where should I go?"

"After you get back on the highway, headed toward Diamond Lake, in about a half-hour you'll come to Highway 97. Take 97 North and, in another half hour, you'll come to a small town, La Pine. Park somewhere in town where you're hidden from the main highway and call me."

"Hunter, what if they find us again." For the first time, Hunter heard fear in her voice.

"Do your best to beat them to La Pine. The county sheriff has an office at the south end of town. Get help there."

"At least you didn't tell me to shoot anybody."

"Uh, you're dangerous enough with a pipe. No shooting unless you have to, AJ. I'll be praying for you and Sam."

"You're full of surprises. A jerk who prays. Thanks, Hunter. I'll be praying that you find us before those goons do."

"So Amazons pray too? That's encouraging. They must even trust a little or my arrival wouldn't be something they would pray for."

"Yes. Sometimes they do pray. Big Amazon prayers."

"See you in about two hours in La Pine, AJ. I'd ask you to give Sam a hug for me, but you're going to be flying low for the next hour or so."

"Hunter, why can't you call the police before you leave and tell them what's happening?"

"Only as a last resort. If I'm correct about who is behind this attempt to get Sam and me, calling the police might completely backfire on us."

Chapter 10

It was nearly one-thirty and still no news from the team Jim and Andy had hired.

Jim sauntered into Andy Rosenberg's office and pulled the door closed behind him. "Have you heard from our friend yet?"

Andy shook his head.

His phone rang.

"Speak of the devil."

The phone rang again.

"You may be right. Better see who's calling."

"Rosenberg here ... That's not good ... Just a minute. Jim's in my office ... Of course he knows."

"It's the Captain, Jim. He says a woman took Jones's girl and ran off with the girl in her car. When he saw her last, she was headed out Crater Lake Highway. She could either go toward Crater Lake or toward Eastern Oregon."

"I can't believe I paid top dollar for a team of elite, ex-special forces. Sounds like they're ex-elites and not so special. And a third party?"

Andy shrugged. "It was your idea and your dollar."

"Mute the phone."

Andy hit the mute button.

"Do you realize how much is at stake here? And now a third party is involved. This is getting way out of control."

"What do you expect me to do about it?"

"Just give me the phone."

Jim punched the mute button. "Is this the Captain?

"Mr. B, you need to hear a few details. Our third party is a young woman who came out of nowhere and got involved. She dented in one of my men's head. He probably has a concussion. I'm stepping in to take his place until he recovers."

"Good. Maybe we can contain all this chaos with you involved. Your orders are changing. We need to eliminate all three, the woman, the girl, and Hunter Jones. Use one of them to get the others if necessary. The quicker this is done the better. Make it look like organized crime is involved."

"Organized crime *is* involved, wouldn't you say, Mr. B? Forget I said that. What if they call in the cops or, worse yet, the Feds?"

"Then you back away, completely. And let Andy know immediately if that happens. I have other means of taking care of that scenario."

"I'm betting the woman will head for Eastern Oregon, maybe Bend. And she'll go to the police when she gets there."

"What's your plan to prevent that?"

"My guys are waiting for me at the fork in the road. I'll be there in a half hour. Then we'll track down this little ..." The Captain launched into some serious verbal abuse of the meddling lady. "If it wasn't for her interfering, we would be discussing the history of Hunter Jones."

"How do you plan to track her down?"

"Do you really want to know, Mr. B? The less you know the less you can be charged with. Just something to keep in mind."

Was the Captain trying to scare him? "You assured me that your phone calls were not traceable back to us."

"That's not quite what I said. You see, the FBI operates this organization called the Data Intercept Technology Unit (DITU) that intercepts all domestic communications. If they got interested in our cell calls, that would not be a good thing. They may not decrypt this call, but they would know who called whom."

"You called Andy, not me. Nevertheless, I will keep that in mind. But you keep your mind trained on that woman who has Mr. Jones's girl. By the way, where is Hunter Jones?"

"I thought you didn't want to know how we were tracking the lady down."

"Jones ... tracking the lady. I see."

"You keep seeing, Mr. B, and you're gonna be a full-fledged member of this black ops team, the team that takes all the risks."

"Just make sure that you do find her, Captain Deke."

"You shouldn't use that name. Remember, to all my friends I'm just the Captain. If you let that name slip while you're in the wrong company, it's you I'll be tracking down."

"Are you threatening me? You do understand who I am, don't you?"

"The CEO of Q-It. I understand who you *are*, Mr. B. And you *do* understand that I can make *that* who you *were*, right?"

Chapter 11

AJ drove away from the small sheriff's office in La Pine at half past two. The office was closed and locked—one of those relationship-building projects that's only staffed when officers are available.

She drove through the town strung out along Highway 97 until she spotted a McDonalds. AJ pulled into the lot and stopped in a parking spot in back of the building, hidden from the traffic on the highway. "Are you hungry, Sam?

Sam hadn't looked up from the phone in her lap for the past five minutes. "A little bit."

"Okay, McDonalds or Taco Bell across the street?"

"McDonalds is okay." She answered while her eyes still focused on the cell.

"What's wrong, sweetie?"

"I'm worried about Hunter. He takes too many chances. He might do something stupid and those men with the guns—"

"Hunter sounds like somebody who can take care of himself. He'll be fine. He can run. That's for sure."

"Yeah." Sam flipped AJ's cell over in her lap for the tenth or twentieth time. "He was gonna try out for our Olympic Team, then Mom died, and he got stuck with me." A tear overflowed her left eye.

"Sam, he doesn't sound like he's stuck with you. From what he's said, you mean everything to him. Sometimes I wish someone thought about me like Hunter does about you."

"Well, if he met you, he might. You're a lot prettier than that woman at church who keeps stalking him. You're beautiful."

"I don't know about that, but stalking? Seriously?"

"Yeah. We go out for dinner after church and she just happens to be having dinner there. We run into her at the grocery story, but I don't think she's really shopping. Not for groceries."

"Does Hunter like her?" She paused and looked into Sam's eyes. "You know, it would be good for you to have a woman around, even if she wasn't actually your mother."

Sam held AJ's gaze. "No, he doesn't like her. But if I had someone to be my mother again, I would want somebody like you."

AJ drew a sharp breath. Now her eyes were welling like Sam's. She looked out the window and brushed an eye before it overflowed. "Thank you, Sam. That was a nice thing to say. The nicest thing anyone has said to me in a long, long time."

"But I meant it."

AJ opened her mouth, intending to answer, but no words came. Only a choking sensation in her throat.

Her cell rang its alert for an incoming call.

Sam flipped the cell over and displayed the caller ID. "It's Hunter's number."

"Answer—"

Sam already had the cell planted in her ear. "Hello."

"Sam, where are you?"

Evidently the speakerphone was on.

"We're at McDonalds in that pine place."

"Did you talk with a deputy at the sheriff's office?"

"I'd better let AJ talk about that." Sam handed AJ the phone.

"Hunter, it's one of those community-relations offices. You know, we're here unless were over there. Call 911 if you have an emergency."

"911. It may come to that if those gunmen locate us."

"Where are *you*?"

"I'm about fifteen minutes from La Pine."

"We've been here less than fifteen minutes. You must be flying."

"Something like that. But I slowed down to make this call. Any signs of the bad guys?"

"No. I think we lost them at the Y. Maybe they're still circling Crater Lake looking for me."

"That's wishful thinking."

Sam reached for the phone. "Can I talk to him?"

"Here's Sam again."

"Uncle Hunter, are you gonna be here in fifteen minutes?

"I think so, sweetheart. You mind AJ until I get there."

"Uh, there's something about AJ you need to know."

AJ studied Sam's face. Where was Sam going with that line?

"She's not a dopehead is she?" Hunter said.

Dopehead?

"Nuhuh. But she's a lot prettier than that stalker, Sally McQuirkle."

"McCorkle. But that isn't saying much, Sam."

AJ grabbed the phone from Sam. "Dopehead? Not saying much? Where do you get off calling me—"

"That's what the service station attendant in Shady Cove thought when you went flying by with tires squealing nearly hitting someone."

"I was trying to get out of Dodge with Sam and me still in one piece."

"But almost running over some little old lady sounds more like a dopehead to me."

"Do read the Bible, Hunter?"

"Quite a bit."

"And you're going to be here in fifteen minutes?"

"In about fourteen minutes now."

"After the day you've had, all that running, I'll bet your tired."

"A little."

"Good. Because I've got a hammer and a tent peg. Wanna take a nap?"

"Ouch. Maybe I should call you JL instead of AJ."

"So you do read your Bible. Even the Old Testament. Amazing. What else do I need to know?"

"AJ, I've got a steel pipe beside me. And it looks like you've got a fly on your forehead."

"Gee, thanks." She paused. "This is a ridiculous conversation. We have two gunmen looking for us, and I've got a little girl beside me who's worried sick about you. And I don't know what I'd do if anything happened to you."

"Glad to hear that you care so much, JL, I mean AJ."

"That's not what I meant, and you know it."

"I'm hoping nothing happens to you, either, especially now that I've found somebody to have such stimulating conversations with."

"Hunter, I've heard that tent pegs can be stimulating to a man's temple."

"Was that some crude joke?"

"You are so—"

"I'll tell you what, AJ. I'll text you a picture of Ms. McCorkle and you can rate yourself against—"

"And I'll tell you what you can do with your text."

Sam grabbed AJ's phone and pulled it from her hands. "Stop it, Hunter. She doesn't know how you tease. She thinks you really mean all—"

"But this time maybe I *did* mean it."

Sam looked at AJ. "He's lying, AJ. Hunter likes you or he wouldn't act like that."

"He doesn't like me, Sam. We've never met, and ... I don't think I like him very much."

"Hence the tent peg." Hunter's voice came through the speakerphone.

"AJ, pick up your phone and turn off that blasted speaker."

"Why should I do that? To suffer more of your verbal abuse?"

"No. Because I think there's a dark-colored SUV following me."

AJ took her phone back and turned off the speaker. "Is it them?"

"I think so. But here's what I want you to do. Get away from Highway 97. It's the main highway in Eastern Oregon. There are too many snooping eyes and video cameras. Does your phone have a GPS app?"

"You mean for maps and directions?"

"Exactly."

"It does."

"Then do a map search for Paulina Lake. Turn on the app for directions. It should give you an option to take some back roads from La Pine to the lake. Nobody will be able to find you, not even James Bratkowski."

"The CEO of Q-It?"

"Forget I said that. Just get you and Sam to Paulina Lake. Meet me at the parking lot for the first campground. You'll see it just as you get to the lake."

"The CEO, Bratkowski? Hunter, is there a high-tech hunting party after us? Is that why you're afraid of video cameras?"

"I'd rather not say just yet."

"Techies aren't violent people. They're not killers."

"I wouldn't bet my life on that right now."

"Hunter?"

"Yes, AJ."

"I'm not a dopehead. I'm not an Amazon, and you would be safe if you took a nap with me."

"I'm not sure that came out the way you meant it, but thanks for the invitation. Maybe I can take you up on it sometime."

She needed to ignore his obnoxious comments and stay focused. "Sam and I will be praying for you. Lose those goons."

Hunter ended the call.

"Sam?"

She looked up at AJ.

"What's at stake that would cause two gunmen to come after us?"

"Maybe it's because Hunter and I are going to see the president tomorrow. He wants to talk with Hunter."

The president?

AJ Scott, what in the world have you gotten yourself into?

Chapter 12

The suspicious vehicle seemed content to remain about a hundred yards behind Hunter's pickup.

At the next straight stretch of road, Hunter slowed, encouraging the SUV to pass.

The driver of the SUV matched his speed and remained behind.

Suspicion morphed to certainty. The goons were following him, and he had to lose them well before he got to Paulina Lake, preferably before he reached La Pine.

Hunter didn't want those men anywhere near Sam and AJ.

AJ ... how had she so quickly become part of his thinking. Sam seemed already attached to the intriguing woman who was obviously more than a warlike Amazon. If Sam had bonded with her as tightly as it seemed, maybe AJ was already a part of his makeshift family.

You are one crazy dude, Hunter Jones. For all you know she's a psycho in desperate need of companionship, a psycho who chose Sam as the object of her sickness.

Hunter squelched the accusing voice. AJ had already proven herself by—by what? Acting like a psycho? Putting a dent in gunman's head?

But maybe she just needed adult companionship and conversation ... like Hunter Jones

No more excursions into ADD. He needed to focus.

La Pine lay only five miles ahead. Maybe he should risk tipping his hand, showing that he knew what the people in the SUV were up to.

Between here and La Pine, there were only a couple of bends in the mostly straight highway. If he made his move now, he would be trying to outrun a late model SUV in his 2002 Dodge truck with a 5.7-liter Hemi for an engine.

He had more power than the SUV, but Highway 97 wasn't the place to use it. He needed somewhere rough, maybe even a place that needed four-wheel drive.

What was the route he'd taken to Paulina Lake? Finley Butte at La Pine, connecting to road 2225, then to Jones Well Road which hit Highway 21 a mile or two below the lake.

Along the way, numerous dirt roads snaked away from the route. They were hardly more than trails, places where four-wheelers went. Good places to lose a vehicle that was more a cross-over utility vehicle than something for off-road exploring.

But he would be tipping his hand when he turned from Highway 97 onto Finley Butte. He needed a quick turn and then the race would begin.

His cell rang.

The caller ID showed AJ's number.

Great! He had only about five minutes until he needed to ditch the SUV tailing him.

Hunter answered.

"We just got to the campground at the lake. We're parked in the parking lot. Where are you, Hunter?"

"I'm approaching La Pine. They're still tailing me, but I've got a plan to lose them."

"If you lose them and meet us here, what then?"

"There's only one way to stop these guys. We have to get their boss to call off his bloodhounds."

"The CEO guy, Bart—Brat—uh—"

"Yeah. Him."

"Can we just head straight for the police after you get here? You know, in a bigger city like Bend?"

"With these guys, AJ, we might get killed trying to reach the police, or even after reaching them."

"Then we'll never be safe."

"That's not so. We just need to focus on ending the danger to you and Sam."

"And to you too, Hunter."

"I deserve trouble for poking my nose into a dangerous environment."

"You really like to skirt the issues, don't you?"

What did she mean by that? Best to ignore it for now. "I guess you're in this pretty deep. So you need to know the whole story."

"When I found Sam, from that moment on, I've been in this all the way. I promised Sam I wouldn't leave her—that I would protect her until she was safe."

AJ was anticipating Sam's needs like a mother would. A lot better than Hunter could. Maybe God had been looking out for Sam, leading AJ to her.

Maybe leading her to you too, dude.

He doubted that. It was a nice thought, but Hunter's lot in life was Samantha Wilson, and he had to be content with that.

There it was again. The distraction of AJ. If he didn't focus, he could get them all killed.

"Are you still there, Hunter?"

"Yeah. Just trying to think of a short version of the story so that you know what we're up against."

"Whatever it is, I'm up for it."

"Are you up for tackling large-scale voter fraud in a presidential election? Voter fraud Q-It style."

"Is that what you've been researching?"

"Among other things, yes. And the only way to keep us all safe is for me to take you and Sam with me to talk with President Gramm."

"So Sam didn't make that up?"

"She told you about our DC trip?"

"Yes."

Sam must have really opened up to AJ. The bond between the two girls, rather the girl and the woman, was becoming something that couldn't be easily undone, unless Bratkowski murdered it.

And what was it the Bible said about bonds? A cord of three strands is not easily broken. Hunter, Sam and AJ. One strand, unseen but braided into the cord via a cellular network.

Somehow, AJ had wormed her way into his life, sight unseen. That shouldn't be possible for Hunter's personality type.

What had Meyers-Briggs labeled him as, an ESTJ? The meticulous, organized, stable, problem solver who guarded what's good and right and who guarded people—rational, logical, a man who lived by facts. And the fact was he didn't know AJ.

She can swing a mean bat and hold her own bickering with you, dude.

"Hunter, where do you keep going? Are you okay? The bad guys aren't—"

"I'm okay. They're still just following me. But back to the president. Once we talk with him and explain what's in my research report, we can ask him to hold a press conference."

"So now the president is at your beck and call?"

"AJ, he called me to go to DC. He must place some stock in me. And this will help him get re-elected, especially after we leak my research findings to the entire nation. That's where the danger to us ends. Don't you see?"

"You think these guys won't risk murder charges once their identity is known?'"

"That's about the size of it. What do you think?"

"I think anyone who thinks they can get the president to cooperate like you just described is probably a dopehead."

Was that the hint of a laugh in her voice? Best not to presume. "I said I was sorry about that, and I explained where that little misunderstanding started."

"But you didn't ask me to forgive you for all the name calling."

"You've really got to balance your books, don't you, AJ? Right down to the last entry in the ledger."

"Hunter, I do forgive you." Her voice had mellowed to a sultry alto. She sounded like the femme fatale in that Sean Connery movie about an insurance—what was he thinking? He had gunmen on his tail, and, in about two minutes, he was going to make a break and run for it.

Somehow, he had let himself fall, sight unseen, for a woman with a sharp tongue and arms that could swing a bone-crushing bat.

Dude, she could be Ms. America or Ms. Piggy. You don't have a clue.

Hunter had tried several times to put a face and a body to that voice. His consensus—five-foot-eight, slender with a wiry sort of strength and enough coordination to have a sweet swing with a bat. Hair resting on her shoulders, dark brown hair. Eyes—hazel or maybe green. A perfectly sculpted face that looked younger than her years. How old was she? She was in grad school, so probably between twenty-three and twenty-five or—

"Hunter? Did we lose the connection?"

No. And it seemed they were making a good one, if he could focus long enough to keep the three of them alive.

"I'm here, AJ. But it's time to put my phone down and do some fancy driving."

"You be careful or so help me I'll—I'll—"

"What? Bash my head in?"

"Just be careful. Sam and I are praying for you."

"Thanks, AJ. If all goes well, I'll see you in about twenty or thirty minutes."

He didn't end the call. His cell was still glued to his ear.

AJ hadn't hung up either. Her steady breathing came through the phone transmitting emotions, the nature of which Hunter couldn't discern.

Were the feelings coming from him or from AJ? Maybe both because, obviously, neither wanted to end this moment, especially since it might be their last conversation.

"AJ, take care because I—I ..."

"Yeah. Me too." She ended the call.

Hunter dropped his cell into a cupholder and then spotted the grocery store at the intersection with Finley Butte. He shifted down but didn't signal.

The SUV came up from behind, only two or three car lengths back.

At the last possible second, Hunter jerked the wheel to the right and stomped the gas pedal to the floor.

Chapter 13

The Captain raced northward on Highway 97 but was still several miles behind his two men chasing Hunter Jones.

Now that they were all out of the mountains, cell service appeared to be continuous along the main highway.

The Captain needed status to plan their next move, so he hit Radley's speed dial number.

"Radley here. Jones just veered off onto a side road in La Pine. We had to turn around to pursue. We can see his dust up ahead, but he's got a big lead."

"Is the tracker still working?"

"Yeah. It's a good thing we decided to put it on his car after we located him and his girl in Shady Cove."

"Yes. So don't do anything stupid like wrecking your vehicle and factoring you both out of the equation. Where are you now in relation to La Pine?"

"About six or seven miles east of La Pine. We just left paved road. We're driving on a dirt road that's turning north."

"Let me get my GPS focused on you." He panned to their area and spread his thumb and forefinger on the touchscreen to zoom in on his men's location. "What's Jones driving?"

"An older Dodge pickup. It's a big four-wheel-drive and I think it has a Hemi in it."

"Like I said, don't do anything stupid like chasing him into rough terrain and crippling your car. Remember, we can catch him later using the tracker. And ... if I was a

76

betting man, I'd say he's heading toward those two lakes northeast of La Pine."

"Which two lakes?"

"Paulina Lake and its twin sister. You two keep tailing Mr. Jones in case his girl isn't at the lake. But I'm going to take the paved highway through La Pine and cut over to Paulina Lake on another paved road, Highway 21. Maybe I can beat Jones there. If that's where the woman and his girl are, I'll nab them. When Hunter Jones arrives, with you close behind, we've got them all."

"Just make sure she doesn't have a bat in her hand."

"Thanks for reminding me."

Fifteen minutes later, Captain Deke approached Paulina Lake. In a couple of minutes, a parking area came into view on his left.

Several cars had parked in the spaces that lined the right side, and a few trucks, with boat trailers attached, sat in the long parking places on the left side. All things considered, this looked like a good rendezvous point, one worth checking to see if it contained a light-colored Jeep SUV.

A light-gray Jeep sat near the road-side edge of the lot. It had some dents in its body and a badly oxidized coat of paint. Maybe it had once been white.

He rolled by the Jeep surveilling it but avoiding any prolonged staring.

A woman sat in the driver's seat.

He circled through the lot and came back, approaching the Jeep on the opposite side.

A short person rode shotgun.

He strained to see inside the tinted windows.

A girl with golden hair.

The girl was key to this whole operation. Get the girl, and they would have Hunter Jones at their mercy.

The Captain unlatched his door with his right hand, and steered in front of the Jeep, blocking it in its parking space. With a tree at the other end of the spot, the Jeep wasn't going anywhere.

He killed his engine, leaped out and pushed his gun against the window beside the girl's head. "Hands above your heads and get—"

The girl's head dropped out of sight.

An explosion of glass sprayed his hands and face. His ears rang. One side of his face went numb, the other side itched from the trickle of blood running from his cheek and forehead.

He dropped to the ground, out of sight of the gun.

The Captain fought through the fog to regain control.

A door slammed on the opposite side of the Jeep.

Who would have guessed the woman and the girl would have the foresight and the guts to respond so quickly. Or that they had a gun. He was lucky to be alive.

With the rest of his crew only a few minutes away, the battle was far from over. The woman and the girl might get away, temporarily, but that was better than Wonder Woman blowing his head off.

Chapter 14

AJ yanked Sam from the driver's-side door of her Jeep.

The gunman hadn't fired yet, but he was only a vehicle width away.

"Stay low, Sam, and run straight into the woods before he spots us."

She took Sam's hand and they ran together while AJ prepared for bullets ripping holes in her back.

But no shots came.

Like two scared rabbits chased from their hiding place, they scurried farther into the trees until the parking area disappeared.

So far, Sam demonstrated surprising running strength for such a small girl. How much farther could she run? A half mile might do if Sam could run that far.

AJ hadn't a clue if her desperate shot had hit the man, but the shattered glass would have sprayed his face. That should have distracted him enough for them to get away without being seen.

With the heavy pistol in one hand, and Sam clinging to the other, AJ ran farther into the trees on the east side of the parking lot.

The forest was a mixture of juniper, fir and pine trees that restricted visibility to twenty or thirty yards. If she could keep their lead, and if Sam could keep the pace, maybe they could lose the gunman.

AJ glanced down at Sam running beside her. She wasn't struggling, more like settling into a comfortable pace.

Running genes must run in Hunter's family. Sam didn't seem to be breathing hard, not as hard as AJ.

Sam looked up at her. "Did you shoot him, even a little bit?"

"I was so scared that I don't know if I hit him or not. Then I pressed something on the gun and it slid open. I can't figure out how to close it, and it won't shoot like this."

"Maybe you already shot him and we don't need the gun."

With their lives on the line, in the middle of a desperate situation, Sam was trying to encourage AJ. How many eight-year-old girls would try to do that for an adult?

Sam was exceptional, and she would be proud to have— AJ had no time for wishful thinking. She needed to focus on ditching the gunman and reconnecting with Hunter.

After ten minutes of alternating between running and walking, they crossed a roadway that appeared to be an entrance to another camping area. The sign by the road said Little Crater Campground.

Sam wasn't running as effortlessly now. Something seemed to be bothering her.

She was a trooper, but AJ needed to give her a break. "We need a place to hide and rest for a few minutes while I call Hunter."

Sam pointed ahead, down the road winding through the campground. "There's a building that looks like a restroom."

"Yes. That's what the sign says. Can't you read it, Sam?"

"No. Can you?"

"Yes. Do you need glasses?"

"I don't know. But I do know I have to go, you know, from getting scared and everything."

"Then we'll use the women's restroom for our hiding place. The campground looks empty, so we should have it all to ourselves."

She led Sam to the restroom, but AJ was careful to stay inside the edge of the forest in case the gunman showed up. She opened the door of the large facility and scanned the inside.

Empty.

She nudged Sam through the door. "You take care of business while I watch for anyone coming."

AJ planted a foot in the doorway to keep the door open a crack. She pulled out her cell and looked at the signal strength. One bar. It would have to do.

She created a new contact, using the last call from Hunter, then pressed the call icon.

"Where are you, AJ?"

It was Hunter's voice, but he sounded like an army drill instructor, minus the four-letter words.

"Sam and I are about two miles east of where I left my jeep, and—"

"Nice of you to let me know about your Jeep. Nobody home. The passenger-side window blown out, right beside Sam's head. I thought—never mind what I thought. Are you both okay?"

"Yes. Sam's fine. She's a good runner. After I shot at the—"

"So *you* shot out that window? Where was Sam when you blew out the window?"

"She was on the floorboard. I told her to get down because that man stuck his gun against the window by her head. *His* gun was pointed at her, Hunter, not *my* gun."

Hunter's breath blasted through the cell's speaker like static. "Sorry for questioning your judgment. Did you hit the gunman?"

"I couldn't tell for sure, and we needed to disappear before he recovered from whatever my shot did to him. We ran. We're hiding in the women's restroom at the next camping area, Little Crater Campground.

"AJ, you should have hidden in the men's restroom. If they look in that campground, the women's room is the first place they'll check."

"You really sound sorry about questioning my judgment."

"I'm sorry, I—"

"You already said that. Besides, men's restrooms are gross, and they're half taken up with things Sam and I can't use. I wouldn't take Sam there. And I've got the door cracked open, so I can see if anyone drives into—uh, Hunter, a dark-gray SUV just pulled in. It's at the far end of the campground. Isn't that the SUV that followed you?"

"Could be. I thought I'd lost those guys. They must have figured out where I was headed. Someone else found you, so there are at least three of them in two vehicles."

"Sam and I need to get out of here. If we head straight south, won't we run across the main road in a mile or so?"

"More like a half mile. I'll leave here and hide somewhere near here for about twenty minutes to let you get to the highway. Hide in the bushes where you can flag me down when I come by. Sam knows my truck, a black 2002 Dodge pickup."

"Sam, you wrinkled your nose at my SUV. Hunter's truck is even older than my Jeep."

"But it's a lot nicer. He takes care of things."

"Meaning I don't?"

"You take care of me just fine."

"And *you* are a lot more important than some clunky old Jeep Cherokee."

"A man beater who drives an old beater." Hunter's voice had lost most of its cutting edge.

"I thought our relationship was beyond insulting accusations."

"Hardly. But at first opportunity, I suggest you and Sam beat it out of there."

"Is he always this annoying, Sam?"

"Only when you don't want him to be."

"Hunter, they stopped at the other end of the camping area. We need to leave now. I can't use the gun. It got stuck open so I can't fire it."

"What is it?"

"Gee, I don't know. A hand gun?"

"Look on the barrel and on the handle. What does it say?"

"Uh, Sig Sauer."

"You just need to push on the slide release and slide it closed on the rails. There's a—"

"I don't have time and it's heavy. I'll hide it here. Gotta go. Take care. I get to see you in about twenty—I mean, see you in twenty minutes, Hunter."

"Looking forward to that, AJ. You be careful too."

AJ and Sam slipped out the door, circled the back of the restroom, and ran into the trees.

South should be a little to the left of where the sun now stood at 4:00 p.m. on a warm June afternoon. Now to avoid leaving a warm trail.

"This way, Sam. Walk softly. Try not to leave any tracks. We don't want to get in another race. These guys have been riding in a car. They have fresh legs."

AJ looked down at the scratches on her legs below the hem of her denim shorts, lacerations from loping through trees and bushes.

Fresh legs. Unlike me.

Chapter 15

The Captain's secure phone sounded its call alert.

He hit the brakes and steered toward the wide shoulder of the highway near the entrance to the campground parking area, where the woman had left her Jeep.

"Captain here."

"This is Bain, sir. When we didn't hear from you, we got concerned. Are you okay?"

"Okay? That depends. I'm not okay with someone shooting me at point-blank range. When someone does that, they'd better finish the job, or I will finish them."

"You didn't run into Jones, did you?"

"No. That wiry witch who's helping him had a gun. When I put mine to the window by the girl's head, the woman shot at me through the glass. I've bled enough from glass cuts to qualify for a blood donation. My earring's gone. She shot off half of my ear lobe. I had to stop the bleeding before I could chase them."

"Sounds like she knows just enough about guns to be dangerous, otherwise ..."

"Yeah. Otherwise. I'm leaving the parking area now. Where are you two?"

"We're at the next camping area to the east. It's called Little Crater Campground. The tracker signal on Jones's vehicle is weak up here, since it has to bounce off cell towers near Highway 97. We lost Jones for a bit and started searching. We knew he'd left the camping area where you are, so we tried the next one. Radley says he's got a signal now."

Voices sounded in the background.

"Looks like Jones is headed east on Highway 21. It goes by East Lake then into Never, Never Land. We're not sure what's on his mind other than trying to rendezvous with the woman and the girl."

"Keep following Jones. He'll lead you to the girl. Then we can take them, find out who they've talked to, and dispense with all three someplace where the coyotes will cover our tracks."

"We're on it, boss."

"Bain, if possible, we want them all alive to interrogate. We can use the girl to force Jones to talk. The witch is a wild card. We'll have to find out what she knows and what her role is. Then we take them all into the back country for one last picnic."

Chapter 16

In a few moments, Sam would be safe beside Hunter, and he'd get his first visual on AJ.

Hunter slowed on Highway 21 and adjusted the cell pressed against his ear. "Describe where you are again, AJ."

"We're behind some bushes by the highway, about a mile east of the first campground."

"I'm almost there. Tell me when you hear a car on the highway."

"I can hear you."

"Good. But don't come out until Sam says it's my pickup."

"She sees you. We're coming out. Maybe this is finally over."

He doubted that but wanted Sam beside him safe and sound. And he was more than a little curious about AJ. Brave, determined, but most of all, she had defended Sam with her life.

The two scampered from behind bushes and stopped on the shoulder of the highway.

Other movement caught his eye. His rearview mirror held the reflection of a dark SUV. The vehicle closed at an incredible rate.

He had to warn and protect Sam and AJ.

Hunter hit the brakes and jerked the wheel hard left.

His pickup turned broadside in the road.

The tires squealed a loud complaint.

But he had blocked the SUV's view of Sam and AJ, who were forty yards ahead waiting for him.

In a few seconds, they could become targets for the gunmen.

He waved them away from the road.

AJ took Sam's hand and pulled her back toward the bushes.

He had only gotten a brief glimpse of AJ, but it was enough to see that she moved like an athlete.

He couldn't let the approaching gunmen have even a brief glimpse of Sam or AJ before they were hidden by the trees. If he did, the two may never escape the gunmen.

Only one option came to mind. Hunter shoved the stick into second gear, revved the big Hemi, and popped the clutch.

The tires squealed as the truck leaped into motion.

Hunter aimed his grill at the grill of the SUV that bore down on him, and he pushed the accelerator to the floor.

* * *

AJ understood the imminent danger to them, but Hunter's maneuver frightened her. He could be killed.

"Run, Sam, and stay in the trees so they can't see us."

The SUV's tires shrieked as it slid to a stop on the road.

A car door slammed.

Someone must be coming after her and Sam.

The men in the SUV probably saw her or they would have gone after Hunter.

"Sam, let's go back toward the campground, but we'll hide in the trees. Maybe Hunter can pick us up there."

Sam didn't reply.

"How are you doing, Sam? Getting tired?"

"I'm okay. Let's keep running. I thought I heard them behind us in the bushes."

"Then we need to lose them. Try to run carefully and not leave footprints. We're going to change direction."

She pulled on Sam's arm and they veered to the left, running almost parallel to the highway. This also let them run on the contours of the hill they were on, rather than continue climbing it. That would give Sam some rest.

Crashing in the brush sounded in the distance behind them. The noises moved toward the lake, perpendicular to their path.

"We've lost them for now." She pulled Sam to a stop. "Let's walk. We'll walk fast but save our energy in case they pick up our trail."

Sam's face held an expression AJ was beginning to learn meant there was something puzzling her sharp little mind, something Sam thought was trouble.

"What's up, Sam?"

"They followed Hunter all the way from that pine town. But they weren't following him when we just talked to him. Then when he came to get us, they followed him again."

"So what are you thinking?"

"I think they know where Hunter is all the time. They can track him. They probably put something on his pickup when we were in Shady Cove."

"And I think you're probably right. Remind me never to play chess with you. But I think Hunter needs to hear this too. I don't think he's figured it out yet, or he wouldn't have agreed to come and pick us up, knowing they were following him."

"But he might have figured it out by now."

"I hope you're right, but I'm going to call him in a minute or two to make sure he knows."

"I don't know if that's a good idea right now."

"What do you mean, Sam?"

"That SUV stopped, and a man got out to chase us. But just before we got too far into the trees to see, the SUV took off after Hunter."

Hopefully, the driver couldn't chase Hunter and shoot too. But what if there were more men in the SUV than the

SLANTED

two gunmen she knew about? Hunter could be in serious trouble.

"It's okay, AJ. You don't have to look like you're about to get grabbed by the monster."

Was she really that transparent? And why were her feelings toward Hunter so strong, almost out of her control?

"You like him, don't you?" Sam looked up and grinned.

"How can I like somebody I've never even met?"

"But you talked with him. Isn't that what people do on dates? They talk and see if they like each other?"

"But they don't insult each other."

"He was teasing ... part of the time."

"Okay, smarty pants. I don't *not* like him."

"But you were worried about him."

"Because I'm worried about you, and we need Hunter to get us safely away from these guys."

"If you say so."

"I—"

A sharp crack sounded a short distance behind them.

"Sam, I think he picked up our trail. Are you ready to run again?"

"I think so. But where?"

"Let's cross over the highway."

"What's over there?"

"Probably nothing but miles and miles of mountains, trees, and rattlesnakes. Lots of places to hide. But we've got to get across the highway without being seen."

Chapter 17

"There's nobody coming down the highway, AJ." Sam pointed diagonally across the road to their left. "Where does that road go?"

"The sign says obsidian flow."

"Odd citizen flow? What is that?"

"I said obsidian. Can't you read the sign from here?"

Sam blinked her eyes, squinted, then shook her head.

"When this is all over, I think we need to take you to see the eye doctor. You might need glasses."

"We?" Sam looked up and grinned.

"It's just an expression."

"But you were expressing that we were like a family... sort of."

"Sam, I would love to have a daughter just like you someday. But if we aren't careful, there might not be any need to see an eye doctor."

"You're just trying to scare me. God will take care of us."

"He has so far, but we've got a way to go. Let's cross over the highway, then we'll circle around that parking area by the flow. Maybe there are some trails we can follow to find a place to hide and call Hunter again."

"I hope Hunter's okay."

The two scampered across the highway and continued into the trees far enough so no one on the highway could see them.

"The signs say the obsidian flow is this way." Sam pointed across the open parking area.

"We'll get there if we follow the trees around the parking lot. We don't want the gunmen to drive in and spot us out in the open."

AJ took Sam's hand and pulled her to the right.

Halfway around the perimeter of the parking lot, the stand of trees narrowed until AJ found herself standing in a clearing with trees on her left separating her from the parking lot.

Sam turned to her right and froze. "Holy smoke!"

"You shouldn't talk like that, Sam."

"Why? I read it in the Bible. Isaiah saw God's holy smoke." Sam pointed ahead.

"There are a lot of things in the Bible we don't normally talk about, unless we have a good reason."

"You mean stuff like *foreign occasion?*"

"You mean fornication? Who told you about that?"

"Our pastor said it was bad. But look, AJ. It's a whole mountain of black glass."

Boulders of obsidian had slidden down the mountain creating a wall of black glass shards. Some shards probably weighed tons, and others one could pick up in one hand.

At every point where black glass reflected the sun back to their eyes, the obsidian exploded into blinding beams of white light. The result, the whole mountainside sparkled like a giant sequined ornament.

Sam scanned the panorama from the trail on their left to where the mountain curved away from them on the right. "Wow. I never knew anything black could be so beautiful."

"Don't you have some black friends who are beautiful?"

"That's different. They're a beautiful chocolate brown."

"If you say so." AJ pointed ahead. "Let's check out that trail. It looks like it has steps that go up the glass mountain. There aren't any people on it right now."

"But it's out in the open on the mountainside."

AJ nudged Sam ahead and they walked toward the trail. "If we can go over this mountain, I don't think they could ever find us."

"But if we get caught here, we don't have any weapons."

"Did you know that the Indians made weapons from obsidian?"

"You mean the *Native Americans*, don't you?"

"When I was growing up, we called them Indians, and nobody had a problem with that. You know something? There are people who like to control other people and so they make rules about words and play stupid games with them?"

"You mean political correctness?" Sam looked up and flashed a mischievous grin.

"You were baiting me the whole time, weren't you? Where did you hear about political correctness?"

"Hunter taught me. But when I tried to teach my friends at school, I got in trouble. My teacher sent me to the principal's office. Hunter had to come and take me home. They call that suspicious."

"You mean suspension?"

"Yeah. I missed two whole days of school all because of Hunter."

"Why in the world would they suspend you for talking about political correctness?"

"It wasn't just that. I think it was more because Hunter called the principal a lizard."

"I don't think he said 'lizard', especially if your principal was on the political correctness police force." AJ laughed.

But how could she be laughing and having a delightful discussion with Sam when their lives were still in danger?

She draped an arm around Sam's slender shoulders and gave her a side hug. "What did Hunter do after he got you suspended?"

He told the principal he was glad I would be at home for two days, because he had a lot of other things he needed to teach me."

"Hunter sounds like a live wire."

"Do live wires hurry out of the room because someone is yelling four letter words at them?"

"I'm sure that happens. Sam, here's the trail. It has steps going up the mountain, above the glass. But..."

"But what?"

"Were you feeding me a bunch of bull just now?"

"Honest, it really happened. But you need to watch your mouth, AJ."

"Why is that?"

"Bull is a four-letter word. Hunter would wash your mouth out with soap if he heard you say it."

"He wouldn't dare."

"You can't stop Hunter if he thinks he needs to do something."

"So he's stubborn?"

"Are we going to go up the trail or not?"

"Come on. Let's hurry. It looks like it will take a couple of minutes to climb to the top, and we'll be in the open."

"Don't you think we should get one of those Indian weapons you mentioned? There's lots of obsidian here at the bottom of the mountain."

"Indian weapons? I thought you preferred Native American."

"No. Native American's what the principal preferred because she was part Indian. That's when Hunter told her if she was Native American, she should get off his land and go back to the reservation."

"This is all true, right?"

Sam nodded. "'Cept for the parts I made up."

AJ mussed Sam's hair. "You are a rascal. Now let's find us a weapon."

"Here's one." Sam held up a piece of obsidian about six inches long.

One end was rectangular, the other like a blade, pointed and sharp along one edge. It resembled a paring knife but had a thicker blade that looked like it could do some serious damage.

A picture formed in her mind of AJ stabbing someone with the obsidian knife. She shivered, erased the picture, and dropped the rock into her side shorts pocket.

"That will be our weapon. Let's climb the steps and disappear over the glass mountain. Then we can call Hunter."

"AJ ..."

"What now, Sam." She pulled Samantha to the bottom step. "You can tell me while we climb the steps."

"You didn't read the sign at the bottom of the glass mountain, did you?"

"No. What did it say?"

"That you broke the law. It said removing obsidian is probated."

"You mean prohibited?"

"Whatever. But you broke the law, AJ."

"You are a chatterbox."

"And you are an outlaw."

"Sam, I couldn't count all the times I broke the law since I found you. They could call me a kidnapper, especially if I took you across the state line. Then I broke the speed limit most of the way here. I passed cars illegally, not to mention I assaulted a man with a steel pipe. Who knows, I might have killed him."

"AJ ... you didn't kill him."

"What do you mean?"

"We had better run up the steps. Look."

At the base of the mountain, not fifty yards away, a man stood. He had a large bandage above his eye, and he held a gun."

"Run, Sam. As fast as you can."

Sam's short legs could only take the huge steps one at a time. It slowed them too much.

Behind them the man steadily closed the distance.

Ahead, the trail seemed to level off. Hopefully, at the top, Sam's legs would have enough left in them to run away from the man while he was still climbing.

AJ glanced back.

A second man emerged from the trees and leaped onto the bottom step.

Sam and AJ needed something to hide them. Something like, "Holy smoke."

"What, AJ?"

"Nothing. Keep running, Sam. I was just wishing for something."

"AJ, he's going to catch us." Sam panted out the words between deep breaths.

"Here's the top. Run hard."

Though the man behind them was still climbing up the steps, they weren't opening up a lead. He had closed to about twenty-five yards, and the determined look on the gunman's face said he hadn't forgotten what she had done to him.

Chapter 18

AJ and Sam's lead over the gunman had dwindled to fifteen or twenty yards.

The trail curved away from the obsidian cliff on their left and ran toward the top of the obsidian mountain which flattened on their right.

AJ scanned the path ahead.

The trail continued to circle back around to—she hadn't noticed on the way up. It reconnected to the trail near the top of the steps. They were running in a circle.

Standing at the intersection was a second gunman.

She glanced behind them.

The man with the bandage above his right eye had closed to within ten yards.

Jagged stones jutted up all across the top of the mountain. The only smooth places where one could run were along the trail.

She and Sam were trapped on the obsidian mountain.

They were out of options. But surrendering to the man whose head she had bashed in didn't seem wise. She chose the second gunman.

"Hurry, Sam. Run hard."

"But, AJ—-"

"I know. But at least we know I didn't kill him with that steel pipe."

"I almost wish you had."

By the time she and Sam approached the second gunman, heavy, raspy breathing sounds had grown so loud that AJ expected to feel the man's breath on the back of her neck.

"Stop! Now! Or she gets it!" Gunman number two pointed his gun at Sam.

AJ leaped in front of Sam and wrapped her body around the girl's small form.

"It's okay," Sam whispered. "They won't shoot me. They want Hunter, and …"

That thought had occurred to AJ too. But did these gunmen place any value on AJ? Or would they just shoot her here in front of Sam?

Please, God. Not in front of Sam.

The man with the bandage on his forehead scanned AJ, inch by inch, in a way that made her feel contaminated. Whatever this man had in mind would not be good.

She had humiliated him and probably given him a concussion. He would want revenge for his wound and his wounded pride.

"Come on, sweetheart. You walk next to me. Real close like." His roving eyes turned her stomach.

"Maybe I don't want to be close to you. You know, you're even uglier with that patch on your face."

Patch head backhanded her.

She partially turned her face and took a glancing blow to her cheek. But her teeth cut the inside of her cheek and the salty, metallic taste of blood filled her mouth.

"Don't do that, AJ. Please." Sam's eyes pleaded with her to not provoke the men.

That was supposed to be AJ's line, correcting a precocious girl who might antagonize them, not the other way around.

AJ spat the blood from her mouth making sure it splattered on patch head's running shoes.

He stepped back out of her range. "It looks like I'm going to have to teach you some manners." He cocked his arm for another slapshot to her face.

"Cool it, Radley." The other man grabbed Radley's arm. "We've got to get these two through the parking area to our SUV. We don't want any tourists to see her and think that you're a wife beater, do we?"

Sam's wide eyes met her gaze. "Please, AJ. Do what they say. I don't want them to hurt you."

Radley chuckled. "The girl's got more sense than you."

For now, she wouldn't provoke them, for Sam's sake. But the evil in the man's eye said nothing short of killing Radley would stop him from hurting her. Pain became a certainty that AJ tried to steel herself against.

"That's more like it." Radley moved close to her side, too close. He jammed his handgun into her back and grinned when she winced. "Come on, sweetheart. We're two lovebirds out for an evening stroll. Play your part and maybe I won't hurt you."

But the expression on the man's face said hurting people was something he enjoyed.

They negotiated the trail down the mountain and crossed the parking area without drawing undue attention.

When they approached the dark gray SUV, Radley pushed her around it and goaded her with his gun to the door opposite the parking area. Now they were out of sight of the few people present.

Radley raised his gun with the butt protruding from his hand.

"Not now, Radley," the other man said.

"When it's time, I get her, Bain. She's all mine. Nobody does what she did to me and gets away with it."

"That will be the Captain's call, not yours," Bain said

So there were at least three men after them, Radley, Bain, and someone called the Captain. If she could contact Hunter, the odds would be even, three against three.

But it didn't take a brilliant deduction to know what was coming. The three would tell Hunter they had Sam. Hunter would go nuts. And he would need AJ to restrain him. If she was successful, the gunmen would kill all three of them.

Radley pushed AJ into the SUV. He took the middle position in the seat and pushed Sam to the spot on his right.

He jammed his gun against Sam's head.

"Ow. That hurt."

"That's nothing compared to what I'll do if my girlfriend here misbehaves."

Bain drove them a short way down the highway, then he turned into a small parking area surrounded on three sides by a dense stand of fir trees. The spot looked like a trail head.

He pulled the SUV in until it was nearly hidden by the trees.

The gunmen had taken her to an isolated location. Was this where AJ would be beaten, interrogated, and killed?

It surprised her that the thought didn't send her into panic. It only brought sadness for who she would leave behind, Sam, who had worked her way deeply into AJ's heart, and Hunter, the phone foe, who had become her phone friend.

Knowing she had no opportunity to see what might lie beyond that cell-phone relationship brought more sadness.

After they all climbed out of the SUV, Bain opened the back and pulled out a small pack and two assault rifles. He slung them over his shoulder and put his handgun against Sam's back.

Radley ground the barrel of his gun into AJ's back and chuckled when she squirmed.

AJ refused to give him the satisfaction of a whimper or a complaint.

"Up the trail," Bain said. "Until we tell you to stop."

AJ studied places where the trees and bushes grew dense along the trail, anything that might help her if she got a chance to escape.

A little more than the length of a football field up the trail, it turned and passed through a small clearing littered with gray, sun-bleached windfalls.

"Stop here." Bain jerked Sam to a stop beside a large windfall.

Radley grabbed the back of AJ's tank top and yanked, choking her.

When he relaxed his grip, she coughed and tried to catch her breath.

"See. I can be a gentleman when I want to."

Bain moved between her and Radley. "Hands high over your head, my brown-haired beauty." Bain gripped her wrist and lifted her arm.

She raised the other arm above her head.

Bain pulled two rectangular objects from the pack. "I'm keeping the receiver." He dropped one of the two objects into a large pocket on his sweats then handed the smaller device to Radley. "Time to wire her and, while you do, I'll tell her the rules."

"There's only one place the transmitter will fit, unless you want to use duct tape," Radley said.

"We don't need any tape. Just make sure it's hidden."

Radley patted her down then stopped when he found her cell in her shorts pocket. He handed the cell to Bain.

"That might expedite things." Bain held it up in front of AJ. "You can have this back in a moment, after I finish telling you the rules."

"The transmitter Radley's holding has a range of 1500 meters. That's about a mile, maybe a little less in this forest.

If we lose contact with you, the golden-haired angel will get a quick trip up the highway to heaven. So I suggest you don't go more than a half mile from the trailhead in either direction."

"Bain," Radley said. "I thought you said the Chinese transmitter was only good for five hundred meters."

"That's the cheap version. This is the Chinese Cadillac version. Plant the wire, Radley."

When Radley slid the transmitter inside her tank top, AJ fought hard to stifle the impulse to knee him in a painful spot.

It lodged inside her bra and from the feel of it, it wasn't going anywhere.

Radley sneered at her as he removed his hands from her body.

AJ stared at the bandage on his forehead then forced a smile onto her lips.

Radley grimaced and drew back a hand to slap her.

Bain grabbed his wrist. "Not now, idiot. She has a job to do."

AJ's heart pounded out the rage she held inside. Maybe she would have another shot at Radley's head, but that would have to wait.

She needed to save her rage for what it would most likely be used for, to sacrifice herself for Sam.

When Radley stepped back after wiring her, AJ lowered her hands.

He shook his head and feigned a frown. "You didn't say the magic words. Say them now, my pretty."

"Magic words? Abracadabra. Poof. Radley disappears."

He gripped her throat with one hand and squeezed. "The magic words are, may I, sweetheart?"

Enough," Bain said.

"Not yet." Radley loosened his chokehold. "Now say the magic words, my pretty."

Bile rose in her throat, bitter and nauseating. AJ spat a mouthful in Radley's face.

He cursed and swung a hand at her.

AJ was ready and ducked under the blow.

Bain grabbed Radley's shoulder and pulled him away. "You've lost it, man. We don't get paid if we muff this job. Stay back. I'll give her the orders."

"Fine." AJ said. "I'm not taking orders from that sorry specimen of a male."

Radley took a step toward her.

Bain stepped in front of Radley and blocked him. He held out her cell phone. "Does your cell still work?"

"It works."

"And you have Jones's number?"

Their plan was becoming clear. She was to lure Hunter to his death using Sam as the bait. AJ was just the messenger, a wired messenger.

She nodded.

Bain gave her the cell. "Call him and set up a rendezvous with him somewhere nearby."

"He's not stupid. He won't just walk into a trap."

"Tell him his girl, Samantha, fell and broke her leg. She needs to be taken to a hospital." He cupped her chin with one hand. "And, when you call him, you need to be a good actress."

"I won't lie to Hunter for you or anyone else."

"One wrong word, one slip of the tongue to Mr. Jones, and I will kill little Samantha in front of you, and I guarantee it won't be painless."

"Don't do it, AJ. They'll kill Hunter."

Chapter 19

"It's already 6:30. You need to call him now." Radley smirked as he held his gun barrel against Sam's head.

Bain shot Radley a disapproving glance. "What do you have for a brain, Radley? The kid might scream or something. If he knows we already have the girl, he might call the police. Then we would have a fine mess on our hands, wouldn't we?"

Bain's redress of Radley gave AJ the courage she needed to push back against these brutes. "I can't lie and act on command, you moron." She glared at Radley.

He pulled the hammer back on his handgun.

The gun clicked.

Sam's eyes widened farther. "Don't call him, AJ. No matter what."

"Shut up, kid, or you'll get a seventy-five-cent bullet in your brain."

"Enough, Radley. Give her a minute to think about it and she'll make the call. If her acting isn't an Oscar-winning performance, we might not get Hunter Jones this evening. And that would make someone extremely unhappy, including little Samantha."

Bain's eyes, as cold as a reptilian predator, met her gaze. "If that happens, you and the girl will learn what real pain is like. The kind that makes a person beg for death. So I suggest you hold a dress rehearsal before you place that call to Mr. Jones."

Instead of replying, AJ took advantage of the awkward moment to walk out of the clearing and start down the trail toward the parked vehicle.

"You're helping them kill Hunter. I hate you, AJ!" Sam's voice grew shrill and piercing. "I hate you!"

Footsteps sounded on the trail behind AJ.

She picked up her pace.

"Just let her go, Radley. She'll call when she's good and ready. But not on your command."

"But what if he calls the police?"

"Then we deserve whatever happens for making a bad decision. But Jones won't call anybody. He'll come. We have him at an extreme disadvantage."

The disadvantage was that their evil had no bounds, but Hunter's morality and ethics did. Was that why evil seemed to win so frequently on planet Earth?

This was not the time to rehash Theology 101. AJ needed to think, to come up with a way to turn the tables on these brutal men.

The murmur of voices from the clearing grew softer.

She couldn't distinguish their words. They were drowned out by Sam's screaming as it replayed in AJ's mind.

I hate you, AJ!

The crack of skin slapping skin echoed through the trees.

Sam's words stopped, replaced by her sobbing.

That's when AJ's tears started, because Bain's evil knew no bounds, not even when a little girl was the recipient.

She should have realized from the beginning how this would end. She should have never gotten so emotionally involved. AJ had never been good enough for anyone to love. At best, she had been like a new toy, something to be enjoyed until people grew tired of her and then abandoned her.

She shouldn't blame Sam. AJ's flaws had caused this result from every relationship she'd had since her parents died. And that would continue until AJ's death, an event that seemed to be scheduled sometime in the next few hours.

Her relationship with Sam was damaged, maybe beyond recovery. That thought ripped her heart.

But what about Hunter? How could she possibly lie to Hunter about Sam?

The answer was simple. She had no other option. But that raised another frightening question. Would Hunter ever forgive her for what she was about to do—sealing the fate of all three of them and killing the message of Hunter's research too?

Why was his forgiveness such a concern?

Girl, don't you even try denying it. You're falling for this guy.

But she hadn't even met him. Besides, none of that mattered. She'd be dead before this day was over ... and so would Hunter and Sam.

AJ didn't deserve Hunter's forgiveness or Sam's love. She deserved what she would soon get, a cruel death at the hands of despicable men.

But what if she could create a wrinkle in the gunmen's plans? And if she were willing to sacrifice her life, maybe there was a way to save Sam and Hunter.

She needed to come up with a plan soon, because the highway lay only a few yards ahead.

AJ stopped at the edge of the road then wiped her tears and her runny nose.

She checked the signal strength. One bar. Should she risk a dropped call from here? That was better than exceeding the transmitter's range and getting Sam killed.

Something deep inside urged her to walk to the bend in the road about two-hundred yards away, out of sight of the trailhead.

After rounding the bend, AJ scrolled through her contacts to the entry she had created for Hunter and pressed the call icon.

Hunter's cell rang once, twice ...

He'd been racing away from the gunmen when she last talked to him, and the goons obviously hadn't caught him, because they wanted her to lure him in. But was Hunter okay?

He answered on the fifth ring.

That's when her sobbing started.

"AJ ... is that you? Are you and Sam okay?"

She tried to reply but her throat constricted and choked off her words.

"AJ, what's wrong?"

She blew out a calming breath and steeled herself for her performance. "Sam fell. I think she broke her leg. We'll have to carry her back to the road."

"Broke her leg? Where are you?"

"About a mile up the road from the campground where I left my Jeep."

"Can I talk to Sam?"

Now what? "She, uh, she's not here. She's back where she fell."

"You left her alone with a broken leg? There are predators in these mountains."

"Hunter, I had to. I didn't have cell reception until I got to the highway. Besides, I needed to flag—" Another sob choked off her words.

Was Hunter getting suspicious? If he was, she needed some distraction. "Hurry. There's a wide spot on the shoulder here where you can pull off the road to pick me up."

"Where are the gunmen?"

"I think they're looking for us by the big obsidian flow. That's where we lost them." It was her second or third lie. She couldn't keep doing this.

"I should be getting close to where you are."

The rumble of a powerful engine came from around a bend in the road.

"I can hear you coming. Now I see you." She stepped onto the edge of the road and waved her hands.

"I see you too." Hunter braked to a stop on the wide shoulder across the road from AJ.

She scurried across the highway and rounded the back of his truck.

The passenger door swung open.

AJ jumped into the big pickup and slid into the passenger seat.

Strong arms pulled her almost into the driver's seat. Hunter held AJ in a fierce embrace.

It felt so good to have protective strength around her, holding her. She collapsed against him and returned his embrace while her eyes overflowed.

She must avoid his gaze. Her eyes would betray her.

"Come on. Let's go get Sam." He released her.

She quickly wiped her eyes.

After seeing Hunter and accepting his comforting arms, she couldn't do this any longer. There had to be a way to warn him.

AJ must choose her words carefully, because the microphone was sending each one back to Bain and Radley.

"Yes. Let's go." She opened the glove box and fished through it looking for paper.

"What are you doing, AJ?"

She needed to shut off this inquisition immediately or she could get Sam killed. "Do you have a first-aid kit?"

"Yes, but it's not in—"

"Oh, it's in the back, isn't it?" She gave Hunter the shush signal and pointed to her tank top, a little above where the microphone was hidden, and prayed he would understand.

Hunter's eyes opened wide. He nodded.

"You need to turn around. Sam's about a half mile behind us."

She pulled out the pen and notepad she'd spied in the glove box and scribbled a short message.

I'm wired. They have Sam. No broken leg.

Hunter drew a sharp breath. "I've turned around. How far is it to where Sam is? Is there a place to park my truck?"

"I'll show you. Like I said, about a half-mile." She scrawled another message.

Drive slowly. It's only 200 yards.

Hunter slowed the truck to near walking speed. "AJ ..." he mouthed the words in silence, "... what are we supposed to be doing?"

She scribbled on the pad again.

I'm supposed to lure you in. They have a gun to Sam's head. I'm so sorry.

Tears blurred the words until she couldn't read them. She turned the notepad for Hunter to read it.

Hunter's jaw clenched, then relaxed. His right hand came off the wheel and rested on her shoulder. "It's all right, AJ. Accidents happen. Don't cry over spilled milk. I've got this, okay?" Hunter had cleverly turned the conversation so they wouldn't have to communicate silently. At least not all of the time.

"It'll be all right, AJ." He took her hand.

Hunter's big hand wrapped around hers then squeezed and, for the first time in several hours, AJ believed it could be all right ... somehow.

My gun!

By the time AJ realized she had blown their one chance to extricate themselves from this situation, it was too late. But Hunter needed to know.

She scribbled out a note.

Blew it. Should have gotten the gun I hid by the restroom.

"Let's not dilly dally. That might put Sam at more risk."

Even in the middle of this ugly, dangerous mess, Hunter was consoling her while the pickup crawled down the road at a snail's pace.

AJ added five or six entries to the asset column for Hunter Jones. But the odds were, she would never be able to cash in those assets. More likely, AJ Scott was about to cash in.

She had corrected all the lies and had no more reasons to hide her eyes, so AJ looked long and hard at the man sitting beside her. Tall, lean, athletic, eyes that radiated intelligence and could change from fierce to friendly at the turn of a word. Only one word came to her mind to describe him, magnificent.

Letting her mind wander like that was dangerous. She needed to get it back in the game they were playing before she let something slip to the gunmen.

The parking spot at the head of the trail was only a few yards ahead. They were out of time for games. From here on, their lives depended on every action, every word spoken, and perhaps on words left unspoken.

"You can turn in at that opening."

Hunter steered toward it and parked. "I'll get the first-aid kit."

"Uh, yes. We'll need it."

The gunmen's SUV wasn't there. Had they moved it so Hunter wouldn't be suspicious, or had one of them left? It was a good thing she had walked around the bend, or she might have been spotted meeting Hunter and would have lost any chance of explaining her lies or of warning him.

She quietly pulled a page from the notebook, kept the pen, and scrawled another message.

Gunmen's SUV gone. May be minus one gunman.

She showed Hunter.

He nodded. "Let's go, AJ. We need to get to Sam before she goes into shock."

They both slid out of his truck and walked slowly up the trail.

She had done her job. There was no reason for Bain and Radley to keep her alive.

AJ waited for either men with guns to accost them or a gunshot that would end her life, whichever the gunmen chose.

She prayed it wasn't Radley making the choice.

Chapter 20

"Don't move! Put your hands on your heads." Radley's voice.

AJ raised her hands to her head.

Had she tossed the paper with her note on it? It no longer mattered except for the punishment Radley would delight in giving her for disobeying.

Hunter dropped the first-aid kit and followed Radley's instructions.

Radley emerged from the bushes on the left side of the trail and circled behind them. "If nobody moves, then nobody gets shot."

He stopped behind Hunter. "Ever so slowly, hands down to your sides and then behind your back. And then be still while I slip on the ties."

"Why would I let you do that? I'd be helpless."

"We've got a genius here. And you're right. But that's how I want you, helpless."

Hunter's hands were still on his head, a head now turned far enough to see Radley. "What if I refuse?"

"We shoot your little girl, Samantha. Then we shoot you."

"AJ, what's this doofus's name?"

"Shut up, Jones." Radley barked out the words.

"It's Radley and I hurt him badly."

Radley jammed the barrel of his handgun into her back. "That's enough of your poetry, you scrawny ..." His description assaulted AJ with a half-dozen of the most degrading names a woman can be called.

She couldn't let him think he was getting to her. Ignoring him was the safest approach.

"Who is this guy, AJ? Boo Radley?"

"Enough word games, Jones. Slip your hands into the ties."

"Maybe you should have brought your partner with you, Boo. Looks like one of us is going to either break your neck or bash in your head again before you can put any zip ties on us."

Crunching noises came from their left. A man stepped out onto the trail. He had Sam clamped to his side with one hand. The other had a gun trained on her head. "FYI, he *did* bring his partner."

AJ looked up at Hunter. "That's Bain."

Sam struggled against the zip ties that bound her hands behind her.

"Sam, are you okay?" Hunter said.

AJ studied Sam's face. A welt discolored her tan cheek.

Bain had done that. AJ leaped toward Bain ready to plant a shoe where it would hurt.

Radley hooked her arm and yanked her back, wrenching her shoulder.

Hunter repeated his question to Sam.

Sam nodded. "I'm okay. After a while you get used to having guns pointed at you."

But Sam had avoided AJ's gaze during the entire exchange. Evidently, she meant what she'd screamed at AJ.

"Hands behind your back, Jones," Radley said. "Or, we shoot the woman. If you still refuse, we shoot your little girl. So what's it gonna be, Jonesy?"

Hunter's hands dropped to his sides and moved behind the small of his back. His shoulders sagged in surrender.

They couldn't just give in to these killers. She had to try something before those ties prevented it.

A two- or three-pound rock lay on the edge of the trail. It would have been perfect to end Boo Radley's terror reign, but the gun against Sam's head stopped AJ from trying for the rock.

Was this their final surrender? Would they be killed now with no chance to fight back?

The urgency of their situation screamed its message through her nervous system.

Do something!

If she assaulted Radley full force, a no-holds-barred kicking, screaming, biting, clawing rage, maybe Hunter could get to Bain.

Before AJ could turn and attack Radley, a message came from a place deep inside of her. It came more like a thought than spoken words.

Wait. Be patient.

AJ's panic subsided.

She'd experienced that still, small voice before and trusted it, because she knew the nature of the One who gave her the message.

Radley jerked her hands behind her, slipped on the ties, and yanked hard until they pinched the skin on her wrists.

She couldn't stifle her sharp gasp but refused to cry out and give Radley any satisfaction.

Within a couple of minutes, AJ, Hunter and Sam, with hands zip tied behind them, were marched up the trail.

Bain stopped them in the small clearing where they had wired AJ. He pulled Sam with him, sat down on a log, and pressed the barrel of his Glock between Sam's shoulder blades.

"You don't have to do that so hard. Hunter can see where your gun is pointed. I think you're just a bully who picks on people littler than you."

Hunter turned toward Sam. "Sam, don't—"

AJ stomped on Hunter's foot to get him to shut up. He would only make things worse. Besides, Sam's annoying the men was buying time whether she knew it or not.

Bain chuckled. "Please grant me forgiveness, your Majesty." He jammed the gun into her upper back.

"Ow! You *are* a bully."

"Shut up kid, or I'll—"

Footsteps sounded from the trail, and a large man strode into the clearing.

"Captain's back," Radley said.

AJ drew a sharp breath as she looked into the face she had shot at through her car window, a face now flecked with dried blood from numerous small cuts. One ear lobe hung deformed and bloody.

His eyes focused on AJ. "You ..." His descriptive names for her were creative but crude. He obviously intended them to be shocking.

She would not cower and give him the satisfaction of intimidating her. "Yes. We meet again. That's such a disappointment. I thought maybe I had let the air out of your head."

The Captain cursed her, reaching further into the dregs of his vocabulary.

She forced herself to take his vile onslaught, and she reflected it back to him with her glaring eyes.

Though AJ hadn't said a word, the Captain's face grew red. "When it's time, witch, you're mine. The taming of the shrew will be my pleasure."

Radley turned toward the Captain. "I've already claimed her for what she did to me."

"Radley, if you let her surprise you with a pipe, you already got what you deserved."

"But you let her shoot at you, point blank."

"That's enough of this nonsense." The Captain focused on Hunter. "We have business to attend to."

"That's right," Radley moved in front of AJ. "We wouldn't want to damage our mic. I need to unwire her." He glanced at the Captain.

"Do it, Radley. But don't dilly dally. We're burning daylight and probably our client's patience."

When Radley's hand plunged inside the neckline of her tank top, Hunter's leg swung in a roundhouse kick.

The kick chopped the back of Radley's knee, sending him sprawling on his face in the dirt.

One of Radley's hands wiped the dirt from his mouth, the other clutched the transmitter that his fall had ripped from inside AJ's tank top.

She didn't even try to hide her smirk.

Radley leaped to his feet and backhanded her.

AJ ducked.

The blow thudded against Hunter's chest.

Hunter's leg kicked upward and caught Radley in the pit of his stomach.

He fell backward, landing on his rear in the dirt. Radley croaked like a bullfrog as he struggled to suck in a breath.

"Enough, Jones!" The Captain had unslung his rifle and pointed the business end at Hunter's midsection. "Maybe Radley had that coming, but this isn't about justice for Radley. It's about the injustice you are doing to our client."

"Don't you mean about Bratkowski's and Q-It's injustice to the United States of America?"

The Captain's jaws clenched. "If there was any doubt about your fate, Mr. Jones, you just removed it. Now I want you to make the long story short, short and to the point. What conclusions were you going to report in your research paper, and who was on the distribution list for this report?"

"If my fate is already determined, why should I tell you anything?"

"You seem to be rather fond of this brown-haired witch."

Radley rose clumsily to his feet, still wheezing from the blow to his solar plexus.

The Captain pointed a thumb at Radley. "Suppose I let him get his revenge for her humiliation—any kind of revenge his little heart desires."

"Don't listen to him, Hunter." AJ's heart had gone from allegro to a presto rhythm. Wait and be patient had sounded good at the time, but now …

This was the moment they had dreaded, the time they wanted at all costs to avoid. There would be violence, maybe horror, then death for AJ, for Hunter, and for Sam.

She looked at Sam whose wide-eyed gaze alternated between AJ's face and Hunter's.

With her hands bound behind her, AJ couldn't even sacrifice herself to save Sam.

Evil would win today. Justice would have to wait. It might have to wait for that final judgment day with the Supreme Judge, the God of the Universe, presiding.

The story of today would end like a bad movie, one with the consummate bad ending, one where the audience walked out cursing the script writers and wishing they hadn't wasted two hours and twenty dollars. But what was being wasted here wasn't time or money, it was three lives.

"Maybe Jones won't cooperate if it's just you, Ms. Witch," the Captain said. "But what if it's Goldilocks who's screaming?" He turned toward Sam.

AJ leaped in front of Sam.

Hunter swung a foot up toward the Captain's face, but he stepped back, then shoved Hunter's foot upward until he landed on his rear in the dirt.

"I seem to have struck a nerve. Sorry, but we're fresh out of Novocain."

Hunter pulled his feet under him and stood. "I can't believe anyone would have absolutely no sense of honor or decency. What *were* you before this, a Ranger or a Navy

SEAL? Were you one of those men, forged by adversity, who said they stood alongside America's finest special operations forces to serve this country, the American people, and protect our way of life? *You*, Captain, are no longer that kind of man."

The Captain winced at Hunter's words which sounded like part of some military creed. Evidently, Hunter had struck a nerve too.

This man might have once been a Special Forces soldier, however, that did not mean the man standing in front of them wouldn't kill them. But did he have the orders and the authority to carry out the killing right here and now?

AJ prayed that he did not. At least that might buy them more time. At this point, every second was precious time, time in which something could change and give them an opportunity to escape.

"Radley, Bain," the Captain called them into a huddle a few feet away.

AJ listened to their muffled voices but could only make out the words "call Mr. B."

She looked up at Hunter. "Did you hear that?"

He nodded. "He wants the permission to kill us, and he wants the associated details to be approved by Bratkowski prior to completing the job."

She lowered her voice "But there's no cell reception here. If he has to make a cell call, he has to drive back down the highway to place a call."

"Let's pray he doesn't have a SAT phone. If he has to drive down the road, we need to take advantage of that," Hunter whispered. "Even if the odds look long. It's our only chance."

Voices crescendoed in the huddle. "Radley you get to snuff the kid. No arguments or you might become collateral damage."

Radley growled something indistinguishable.

"It's almost seven thirty, I'll make the call now." The Captain pulled out his cell. "No service here. But there was back at the camp. I'll be back in a few minutes. You two, watch those three, and stay away from Hunter's feet."

The Captain strode down the trail.

How long did it take to walk to the car, drive to the campground, make a call, and return? Ten minutes? Maybe fifteen if the call took a while?

What they did in the next ten to fifteen minutes would determine if Sam, Hunter and AJ lived or died. And the only thing they had going for them was that Bain and Radley might be reluctant to kill them before the Captain returned after making their final arrangements.

Please, God. There's no more time for waiting patiently.

Chapter 21

At 7:30 p.m., the Captain pulled into the campground at the west end of Paulina Lake and stopped in a parking spot near the road.

His cell showed about half the bars. The signal was strong enough. He didn't want a dropped call when he was discussing important business, business like disposing of bodies so they didn't become evidence that could be used against him for murder charges.

Officially, Andy Rosenberg was his contact, though the Captain wouldn't do anything unless explicitly approved by the man paying him, Bratkowski. Using Rosenberg was probably Bratkowski's way of distancing himself from the unsavory details of this inconvenient predicament caused by Hunter Jones.

He keyed in Rosenberg's number.

"Rosenberg here."

"This is the Captain. We have the three requisitioned items. Before we pass the point of no return, I wanted confirmation on their disposition."

"Three you say? Weren't only two ordered?"

"Yes. But, as it turns out, there are three. Does that make a difference?" If it did, he would ask for more money. After all, there was more risk with each body.

"Uh ... maybe I should get Mr. B's take on this before proceeding."

So Rosenberg was squeamish about killing a kid. "Yes. Maybe you should get his take." *You gutless wonder.*

"Hang on while I get him."

One minute ran on to two, which soon became five. Then came the sound of a door closing.

"What do you want, Captain Deke?" Mr. B's voice.

"In case you've forgotten, to you it's just the Captain."

"Okay, Captain. Why are you calling?"

"We have the troublemakers, all three of them. Just wanted confirmation that I understand your orders before I do anything that's irreversible."

"You are the expert in irreversibility. Why are you asking me?"

"I'm making sure that the irreversibility applies to all three, including the smallest one."

"It does. How could it not? And when you're done, take them somewhere in the back country and let nature take its course with coyotes, buzzards and whoever else is on the clean-up crew. Do you understand, oh Captain, my Captain?"

Deke chuckled. A geek who knows poetry. "So then, the bleeding drops of red?"

"Yes, all three, fallen cold and dead."

"And so shall it be." Deke blew out a sigh. "It's a shame though."

"You're not backing out on our agreement, are you?"

"No, Mr. B. It's just that the woman is a beauty, like one in a thousand. And the girl, she's bright. Maybe one in ten thousand. Mr. Hunter Jones—I will enjoy putting an end to his miserable existence. That's all I needed to know."

"Then you know your orders. Carry them out, now."

Bratkowski ended the call.

"You didn't tell me, Mr. B, who gets the nasty task of sending the little, golden-haired angel off to angel land." He smiled. "So I choose Radley."

Chapter 22

Over the past few minutes, Hunter concluded that Sam had been systematically avoiding AJ. Sam was full of positive energy. She never gave off bad vibes, but the air around her was full of them.

Something must have happened before AJ left to rendezvous with him. But Hunter had no time to devote to that mystery, because the three of them had little time left to live if they didn't take some action soon.

"What are they going to do to us, Uncle Hunter?"

"Sam, what's the worst thing they could do to us?"

"They might kill us."

"Suppose they kill you. What happens then?"

"I go to heaven."

"And who will you see there?"

"Mom and Dad ... and Jesus."

"That sounds pretty good to me."

"But I want to be here with you and AJ."

AJ's head whipped around, and her eyes focused on Sam.

Sam's eyes overflowed as she met AJ's gaze. "I'm sorry, AJ. I—I didn't mean it. Really."

"It's okay, Sam," AJ leaned toward her. "Heaven would be great, and I cancelled my reservation to the other place a long time ago. But, unless these guys change their minds about God, that's where they're going, you know, to the other place."

"Let's not give up on life here on planet Earth just yet. There are a couple of people around here I'd like to spend it with."

AJ's head turned toward him. "If that was a proposal, Hunter Jones, it's a fine time to be proposing. Besides, it was lame. About what you'd expect from some data geek."

"What makes you think I'd propose to someone I only laid eyes on an hour ago?"

"You were laying the words on pretty thick before that."

"Oh? What did I say? Take care, I'll pray for you?"

"There was a lot more than that going on and you know it."

"I told you he was clueless about girls," Sam said.

"I may have gotten a few clues today," Hunter said. "But none of that matters unless we can get out of this situation."

"It never really matters with someone like me. Never has and ..." AJ looked away. The one eye he could see welled and then overflowed.

First, Sam was crying. Now AJ had started. What was going through her mind? If they were going to attempt to escape, they needed a positive outlook, not pessimism.

"AJ, what did you mean by *someone like you*?"

"Nothing. Forget it."

They might not have long to live. This was no time for misunderstandings. "Do you mean someone who risks their life for the most important person in the world to me." He looked down at Sam. "And you've seen what I can be like. So the real question seems to be, who would want someone like me, the person responsible for our situation?"

"From what I've seen and what Sam's told me, I would."

She would? Was that a yes to his lame proposal?

There was too much happening here to let life simply slip away. Hunter lowered his voice. "Then I suggest we make a plan for ditching this place." He tried to smile at AJ, but smiles were hard to come by right before a person's execution.

Bain and Radley had been huddled about fifteen yards away discussing something in low tones for the past five minutes.

Bain turned toward them. "That's enough talking from the inmates."

"Yeah. No one has escaped from death row in over thirty years, so don't get any ideas," Radley said.

The two resumed their discussion, occasionally glancing at AJ and smirking.

Whatever the two were planning did not bode well for AJ.

Chapter 23

Bain and Radley had forced all three of them to sit on the ground. Probably a move to take away the kicks he had used on Radley.

Hunter leaned close to AJ. "If we could free our hands and jump them, with surprise on our side, we might be able to get away before the Captain gets back."

"I forgot to mention it, but I have a piece of obsidian in my shorts pocket. It's shaped like a knife. They stopped searching after they found my cell."

"Is it sharp?"

"Uh, I've been afraid to move the wrong way. It might cut through my shorts."

"Sounds like it'll work, but not with our hands zip-tied behind us. We need them in front."

"I can get them to tie my hands in front," Sam said.

"Sam, we can't give away our plans."

Sam worked her knees under her. "It'll work. You'll see." She rose to her feet. "I need to tee tee!"

Radley sat on a log and ran his fingers across the bandage above his eye, where AJ had split open his head. "Nobody's stopping you, kid."

Bain sat down beside Radley, turned his head her way, and glared. "Do it, but I don't want to hear about it."

"Fine." Sam walked toward Radley who was perched on the log with his legs stretched out in front of him.

She stopped when she stood over Radley's foot. "You said nobody's stopping me."

"Sam, don't," Hunter said.

"If she had her hands in front of her, maybe you wouldn't get a wet shoe," AJ said.

Radley realized the danger and pulled his feet back to the log. "Holy—kid, didn't anyone teach you anything?"

Sam looked up at Radley. "Didn't anyone teach you anything, like you shouldn't point guns at people?"

Radley pulled out a knife from his pocket.

Sam tried to back away.

He hooked one of her arms and spun her around.

"I'm sorry. I didn't mean—"

"Hold still." He grabbed one of her hands and, with a deft motion, sliced the zip tie.

"Can I—"

"In just a minute you can." He pulled another zip tie from his pocket, clamped Sam's wrists together in front of her, slipped in her hands, and cinched the tie tightly around her small wrists.

"Use the bushes over there. But don't try running away. And you'd better answer if you hear me calling you, or you won't like what happens."

"Radley," Bain said. "That kid can run. You saw how fast Blondie and the babe disappeared, and we couldn't catch them."

"That's because we had to track them. The kid can't outrun me."

Sam turned toward Radley and waited for him to look up at her. "Wanna race me to the police station in that pine town?"

"Like I said, you try anything, and you won't like what happens to you."

Radley had just threatened *his* girl. When the time came to jump them, Hunter would remember what the man said. When a person attacks a brutal captor, there's little room for mercy. Radley would get none from Hunter.

When Sam emerged from the bushes, Hunter knew her little trip was too short for a girl's tee tee excursion. Hopefully, their captors would be clueless, because closer scrutiny was the last thing they wanted during execution of the next part of their plan.

Sam returned and snuggled against AJ's side.

While Bain and Radley discussed something from their seats ten yards away on the log, Sam slipped a dark object, about six inches long, from the side pocket in AJ's shorts.

Sam leaned her head on AJ's shoulder and slid her bound hands behind AJ.

The scene looked innocent, like a young girl getting comfort from her mother.

But Sam wasn't acting. Despite their one misunderstanding, the bond between these two had grown strong in only a few hours. The danger and risks taken for each other had welded two lives together.

What was he going to do about that? Sam couldn't handle another loss, especially of a mother figure.

Mother figure … it would have been an interesting possibility to explore if he had time, but …

Hunter tried to relax his rigid body and lean back to look behind AJ.

As he slumped backward, AJ's hands fell apart behind her. The rest of her body remained still, until AJ slid closer to him. Her arm touched his and slid an inch or two behind it.

Bain rose to his feet and turned toward them. "I wonder what's keeping Deke."

AJ's arms and body seemed to freeze.

"He's the Captain to us." Radley stuck out a thumb at his three captives.

"Even if they heard, those three don't matter. They won't be—"

"Enough, Bain," Radley said.

"I don't think I want to hear the details of their plans for us," Hunter whispered to AJ. "But we need to hurry."

She slipped one hand behind him. Her fingers ran across his wrists. In one quick motion she cut the zip tie.

It had to be a sharp piece of obsidian. That shouldn't surprise him, because the Indians had used the tempered volcanic glass for knives and arrowheads.

The obsidian knife was all Hunter had. It would have to do.

Bain, still on his feet, turned toward the bushes where Sam had gone a few moments earlier.

"Think I'll take a short walk," Bain said.

"Are you gonna tee tee?" Sam said.

"Grown men don't tee tee, squirt." He shook his head and walked into the bushy area.

AJ shifted the obsidian knife to her other hand and cut Sam's ties. "Keep your hands together, Sam," she whispered.

Radley looked their way. "Knock it off. That's enough talking."

AJ put the knife in Hunter's hands.

This was the moment they had waited for. With Bain temporarily out of sight, they had only a single man to overcome.

Hunter nodded toward AJ, then adjusted the obsidian stone in his right hand so he gripped the handle portion.

The sharpest part seemed to be almost three inches long. That could do a lot of damage.

AJ slowly slid away from Hunter.

"Stop moving over there or I'm going to stop you." Radley stood.

AJ ignored Radley's command, and she slid across the ground farther from Hunter.

Hunter glanced toward the bushes. Still no sign of Bain.

Radley strode toward AJ. His path would take him near Sam and only a couple of feet from Hunter.

He put his shoes flat on the dirt and placed his hands on the ground behind him, ready to push up to his feet.

If only Radley would—

Sam stuck out her foot and hooked Radley's ankle.

His momentum spun her around on the ground.

Radley stumbled forward, flailing to recover his balance.

Hunter attacked Radley's right side.

He buried the knife blade deep in the man's face, near his eye.

Radley dropped his rifle. He screamed and clutched his face with both hands.

AJ had picked up a heavy rock in one hand.

She drove it down hard on Radley's head.

The dull thump stopped Radley's screams. He lay still.

Hunter grabbed the man's gun.

It looked like an AR-15 with a bump stock. He understood the modification to the gun, but Hunter had never shot one. That would probably change in a few seconds.

"Take Sam behind those trees." He pointed to his right. "Stay there until I join you."

AJ gripped his arm and met his gaze. Fear shadowed her beautiful face. "Be careful, Hunter."

He nodded, then turned toward the gap in the bushes where Bain had disappeared.

At somewhere around 8:30 p.m., the twilight was still bright. Too bright.

Twigs snapped ahead to Hunter's left.

After the scream, Bain would probably emerge from a different spot, ready to shoot anything that moved.

Hunter raised the AR-15 to firing position.

Branches on the bush wiggled.

Before Hunter could react, a spray of bullets mowed down a bush beside his right arm.

He pulled the gun into his shoulder, aimed at the movement in the bushes, and squeezed the trigger. The gun came alive in his hands, jumping in a staccato of cracking sounds.

Hunter's aim was off to the right.

He leaped to his left, away from Bain's last volley. Hunter squeezed the gun more tightly, then aimed and fired a long burst.

Bain fell from the bushes and landed on the ground. He groaned but he didn't move.

The sound of a vehicle slowing came from the direction of the parking area one-hundred-fifty yards down the trail.

The Captain. But had he heard the shooting?

Best to assume that he had.

Hunter ran to Bain.

Blood pooled near the man's midsection. He was badly wounded, incapacitated.

Hunter scooped up Bain's rifle and ran to the trees where AJ and Sam waited.

"Thank God you're okay."

Hunter shoved Bain's AR-15 at her. "Let's go. This way." He pointed westward, away from the Captain, toward the lingering glow of the sunset that still lit the western horizon.

"We need to move fast. The Captain just drove into the parking spot."

Hunter had no clue if the Captain, inside a vehicle, could have heard the shooting.

He pulled AJ to his right and started running westward through the trees.

AJ ran with him, the AR-15 in one hand and Sam's hand in her other.

The three of them would not be able to outrun the Captain. And at somewhere between eight and nine o'clock, it was still light enough for him to pick up their trail.

Dude, running may not be wisest thing to do.

Hunter hooked AJ's arm and pulled her to a stop.

"What are you thinking? We need to get out of here."

"AJ," he whispered. "Be ready to shoot if it comes to that, but you stay here with Sam. We have him outnumbered and outgunned. It's time for us to stop running. I'll be right back."

He turned back toward the trail.

"Uncle Hunter, don't go."

"Sam, stay with AJ until I get back. I love you, Sam." Why had he added those words? She might think he wasn't coming back.

Dude, that's a real possibility.

Chapter 24

Hunter stepped on a dry twig, intentionally.

The sharp crack echoed through the trees.

He walked through an area of dry leaves, sending crunching noises through the forest.

Would the sounds divert the Captain's attention and keep him from running to where his men lay? If not, he would soon discover that Hunter and AJ were armed and loose in the wild. They would lose the element of surprise. With a man like the Captain, that loss could mean their lives.

Hunter reached the trail but remained a few steps back in the bushes. After he had retreated fifty yards along the trail, still seventy-five yards or more from Bain and Radley, he crept to the edge of the trail and waited behind a young, bushy pine tree.

Footsteps came from the direction of the parking spot. But the Captain didn't appear.

Soon the footsteps stopped. Evidently, the Captain had grown suspicious, reluctant to run into an ambush.

Hunter raised his rifle to firing position and peered through the bush, studying the trail for any signs of movement.

"Drop your gun or I'll drop you." The raspy voice came from behind Hunter.

He'd been too careless, and at this juncture, there was no reason for the Captain to wait.

Hunter dropped his weapon and balled his fists while he waited for bullets to rip into his body.

Please, God, keep Sam and AJ safe.

He lurched forward when a burst of gunfire came in a staccato of sharp cracks.

The Captain grunted something indistinguishable and pitched forward, landing hard on the ground.

When Hunter looked across a small clearing, AJ sprinted toward him. Sam trailed a few steps behind her.

She had disobeyed him.

But what if she hadn't?

AJ dropped her rifle and leaped into his arms.

She clung to him, her heart pounding against his chest.

At that moment, death's icy chill exploded into exhilaration.

When he looked down into the tear-streaked face of the woman who had just saved his life, only one action seemed appropriate. Hunter leaned down as AJ's head rose up to meet his.

It was a bruising collision of a kiss that didn't last long.

"Ouch," AJ said in a raspy whisper. She clasped her hands behind his neck. She gently pulled. "Can we try that again?" Her voice had dropped to a low, sultry alto that he couldn't refuse.

His free arm wrapped around her. "I thought you'd never ask."

"Yeah, do it, Hunter." Sam's voice. "That man's not moving. I don't think he's gonna move again, ever."

From what he'd already seen, and from Sam's judgment, Hunter chose to forget the motionless body for a moment. He relaxed and let AJ guide him to his target.

When he kissed AJ, it seemed she put her heart and soul into that kiss. Maybe it was the adrenaline still coursing through their bodies. Or maybe it was the charge that had been building up between two willing conductors until the voltage pressure discharged across the gap in a sizzling bolt of lightning.

Regardless, that discharge could never have occurred during a cell phone conversation, though that's where the pressure had started building.

When she looked up at him afterward, the evidence said there was a lot more than adrenaline behind that kiss.

She unclasped her hands and cupped his cheeks. "All that time we spent talking on our phones, I kept wondering what sort of man was on the other end of the call."

He studied her eyes in the twilight. "Did you get your answer?"

"Yes. A good man. The best."

"And I wondered about Amazon Jane too. It seems she's more like Amazing Jane. Certainly not Plain Jane. But I need to check on this Captain guy you saved me from."

AJ released Hunter and picked up her rifle. "I don't know how I did that. Without hesitating, I—I killed someone."

Hunter knelt beside the still body. "Yes you did kill someone, someone sent to kill us. But I don't think these guys realized who they were up against—a brilliant almost-nine-year-old girl who could trip up their plans. Then there was Amazing Jane and—"

"And a world-class runner, according to Sam."

A distant wailing noise echoed through the trees.

"Do you hear what I hear?" Hunter said.

AJ turned her head toward the west. "Well, it's not a song high above the trees. It sounds like a siren. Maybe more than one."

Sam stood near the Captain. She studied his AR-15.

"Sam, don't mess with his gun. I'll take care of it. But you and I, AJ, need to decide what we're going to say to the police ... so they don't arrest us."

"Don't you think we should walk down to the road to flag them down?"

"Yeah. But first ..." Hunter trotted over to where the Captain lay and scooped up his gun. He patted the man's pockets and pulled out a handgun. "All guns need to be accounted for when we meet the police down by the road. My wrists are sore enough. I don't want any more cuffs on them, especially police handcuffs, the kind you can't cut off."

AJ looked his way as they strode down the trail. "What should we tell the police? You know, I'm not even sure why all this happened."

"AJ, here's what the police are going to see. Bain is too badly shot to do anything. Radley has a stab wound by his eye, and he has a cracked skull. He's completely incapacitated. The captain was shot to death. When they ask us what happened, that's what we're going to tell them right after we give them all the weapons."

"They'll want to know why," AJ said.

"We'll say it's because those three were sent to interrogate us and kill us."

AJ nodded. "But then they'll ask us who sent them."

"We say it was somebody at Q-It."

AJ met his gaze. "I would like the next question answered too. They'll ask why someone at Q-It would send killers after us?"

"And I'll say because of my imminent research report which might incriminate people at Q-It."

AJ's eyes widened. "So that's what this is all about. Can you prove all that is true?"

"And that's exactly what the police will ask. Then I'll say get the Captain's cell phone and see who he went to call a few minutes ago. In that call, he likely got permission to kill us. That phone call should lead them to the man running this operation at Q-It."

He grinned at her. "You'd make a pretty good cop, AJ. For certain a pretty one."

"What if they try playing good cop, bad cop with us, trying to get us to say the wrong thing?"

"I'll tell them these men kidnapped my girl and my girlfriend, so I took them all out."

"When did I get promoted to girlfriend?"

"Sam promoted you, and I could never say no to my girl."

"So my promotion came from Sam?" AJ's forehead wrinkled into a cute, contrived frown.

"No. You earned Sam's trust and I—well, you see how it is with Sam and me. We come together as a package."

Sam moved to AJ's side as they stepped onto the shoulder of the road. "Can't we all be together in one package?"

The wailing of the siren grew piercing.

AJ cleared her throat. "Save that for another time, Sam. That police car should come around the bend any second now."

The first police car screeched to a stop in the early twilight and pulled onto the shoulder of the road about thirty yards away. A young officer slid out, weapon drawn, using his car for protection. "Police! Put down your weapons and put your hands on your heads!"

Hunter had already piled the weapons at his feet. "Weapons are down, officer," Hunter called out. "Sam, hands on your head."

"Even the kids have to?"

"Especially the kids. We don't want any more shooting, do we?"

"All right." Sam's tiny hands clasped on top of her golden curls.

"Speaking of shooting ..." the young officer said as the second police car came to a stop. "We have reports of gunfire. The call center said maybe automatic weapon fire."

"AR-15s with bump stocks," Hunter said. "That's what they brought to kill us with."

"Who are *they* and *where* are they?"

The second policeman, a muscular, middle-aged cop, moved to the young officer's side.

Hunter looked at AJ.

She turned toward him and nodded. It was his cue to start the script they'd rehearsed minutes earlier.

"There were three killers. Two are wounded seriously, incapacitated, about two-hundred yards up the trail. The third is dead about a hundred yards up the trail. I had to shoot him."

AJ shot him a laser look. "No. He didn't, officer. I shot the third guy, because he was about to shoot Hunter. He's only trying to protect me."

"We'll sort that out later. First, they're all dead or incapacitated? You sure about that?"

"Positive," Hunter said. "Here are their weapons. Well, the two incapacitated men might still have handguns."

The two policemen circled the car they'd been using for protection and strode toward them.

The young guy arrived first and stopped a few paces in front of them. He studied the guns on the ground, then focused on Hunter. "So a girl, a young woman, and a somewhat capable looking man, all without weapons, took out three hired killers?"

"I didn't say we didn't have weapons," Hunter said.

"I had a gun to start with, but it jammed," AJ said.

"And we had the obsidian knife," Hunter said.

"And I tripped the big guy when the other one had to go tee tee," Sam said."

The young officer turned to the older one. "You buying this, Rodriguez?"

"All I can say is, if one of us has to go tee tee, the other one had better be on guard."

"You should never underestimate a bright eight-year-old or a young Amazon warrior." Hunter looked at AJ.

Her smile was back. Things were looking up.

The two policemen searched them and seemed to relax a bit when they found no weapons.

"I'll call for the ambulances," Rodriguez said.

A third cop arrived while Rodriguez was on his radio. Then the detailed questions began.

Soon a state trooper arrived. He and the third cop went up the trail where Bain, Radley and the Captain lay.

Though the sun had set over an hour ago, on the east side of the Cascades, the long twilight of late June gave plenty of light for the police to find the men and assess their wounds.

After Hunter provided ID, the young officer's eyes widened. "Are you that professor, the data guru who was on YouTube a few days ago?"

"I'm not a professor. But, yes, that was me and that's what this attempted murder today is all about."

"Hey, Rodriguez, it all makes sense. This is the dude who's about to reveal the goods he has on Q-It. It might put them out of business."

"Not out of business. More likely just a changing of the guard," Hunter said. "But it's why we've got to catch a flight at 6:00 a.m. in Medford. We've got a 5:00 p.m. appointment with President Gramm tomorrow in DC."

"That's not likely, Jones," Rodriguez said.

"Once you let me make my one phone call, it's highly likely, if you want to keep your badge."

"You don't say," the younger officer raised his eyebrows in mock surprise.

"*I* don't say, but the president's Chief of Staff, Mr. Jeffrey Montgomery, will say. He set this meeting up for the president."

"Yeah," Sam said. "You don't even wanna make the president mad, or he'll nuke you."

"Sam, where did you hear that nonsense?"

"You said that's what he should do to Q-It."

"That was figurative speech."

"I can figure too. Besides you owe me a vacation and we're gonna have one in Washington DC."

"Enough!" Rodriguez bellowed. "We'll see what we can do to help. But you have to stay a while longer until we finish our investigation. The crime scene crew should be here in a few minutes to begin theirs. We'll need you here for part of that."

"The stakes are high in this meeting with the president. Every American will be impacted. You've got to do better than 'I'll see what we can do'."

Rodriguez sighed out his frustration in a sharp blast. "I'll call for the police chopper. It can get you to Medford in about thirty minutes. It'll cost me an hour or two of paperwork and some other harassment. Now, can we count on your cooperation, Mr. Jones?"

He nodded. "Here's my card. It has my contact information. You have all the guns. AJ and I each shot once so you can scrape our hands or whatever you—"

"The CSI team has adhesive discs for GSR collection, gunshot residue. The team will be here in about thirty minutes. They'll do their work, and we'll have you out of here shortly after that. You'll be home before midnight."

Rodriguez was good for his word. Shortly before 10:30 p.m., Hunter, AJ and Sam boarded the helicopter on the roadway near the parking spot.

Hunter slid in the rear seat behind the pilot. "We need to make a stop on the way to my house."

"They didn't authorize that. No one told me."

"We need to get to the Walmart Superstore in Eagle Point before it closes at midnight, because Ms. Scott needs to buy some clothes for a visit with President Gramm tomorrow."

"The president? And you're shopping at Walmart for clothes for a White House visit?" The pilot rolled his eyes then focused on AJ. "Maybe you should just click your heels."

"Maybe you should just put your hands on that stick and take off now," AJ said. "We've got a long way to go, a lot farther than Kansas."

"Okay. Eagle Point in twenty-five minutes. And FYI, we didn't stop there. It never happened. Got it?"

"Eagle Point? Never heard of the place," AJ said.

Chapter 25

Why hadn't the Captain called. It was after ten o'clock.

Jim strode through the open door of Andy's office. "Did the captain give you his final report on the disposal of the, uh, merchandise?"

"I haven't heard anything since he called us around 7:30."

"You don't suppose he balked at the kid, or maybe something else, do you?"

"Jim, you talked to him, not me. Did you detect any reluctance to finish the job?"

"No, it's just that I have this feeling that something went wrong, or we would've heard from him before now. Finishing this job is not the kind of thing he would drag out. You get it over with and you get out before something does go wrong."

Andy leaned back in his chair and a shadow seemed to pass over his face. "Suppose something did go wrong. What's the worst we might have to deal with?"

"The worst-case scenario ..." Jim laughed. "Hunter Jones kills all three ex-Special Forces warfighters, releases his report, and we have the DOJ on our backs. Then we're subpoenaed and forced to attend inquisitions by the House and Senate Judiciary Committees."

"Like that could really happen."

"What would you do if something like that did happen, Andy?"

"I'd probably stick around, get a good lawyer, and look for an opportunity plead out."

"But you are an accomplice. You knew all about the plan to eliminate three people and you participated in it. At a minimum, that's conspiracy to commit murder."

"You've become one of the wealthiest people in the world. What would you do, Jim?"

"Always plead innocent. Never plead guilty, and never take a plea bargain if it admits guilt. Get the best legal team money can buy and fight the attacks every step of the way. Find somebody else to blame, either a business competitor or a disgruntled employee ... or a guilty employee."

"You mean you'd sell out your own people?"

"Rosenberg, I've invested too much in this company to give it all up, especially to the likes of some data analyst like Hunter Jones."

"Does that mean you'd sell me out?" Andy's tone had turned to a whiny complaint.

Maybe Andy believed he *would* sell him out.

If he believes it, he'll act on that belief no matter what I tell him. And he did develop the algorithm we use. So ...

"Nah. You know I'd never do that."

Chapter 26

From the time they boarded the helicopter, at 10:30 p.m., it was a race with time to reach the Medford airport by 5:30 a.m. for their six o'clock flight to DC.

About five minutes after takeoff, Hunter remembered that the crime scene crew was busy checking out his pickup.

How would he, Sam, and AJ get to the airport in the morning? He could call Zach. But Zach would probably be sleeping when the three of them arrived at Hunter's house around midnight.

And what about *their* sleep? They would have to get up at 4:30. He could make it on four hours of sleep, but AJ looked exhausted. And where would she sleep in his two-bedroom house?

Having AJ sleep with Sam would never work. Sam might be an enchanting eight-year-old Goldilocks while conscious. But once asleep, she turned into an arm-slinging, leg-kicking monster, who usually woke up in the morning crosswise in her bed.

After Sam's mother died, Hunter had often fallen asleep on Sam's bed while she cried herself to sleep, only to be awakened with those tiny but powerful feet shoving him off the six inches of mattress left after Sam turned crosswise.

AJ nestled against Hunter's neck, then turned her head to speak into his ear, her voice barely audible above the incessant wop, wop that was giving Hunter a headache.

"You're not even trying to sleep. What are you thinking about?"

He leaned his head toward her ear. "Uh, I'm wondering who you're gonna sleep with at my place tonight."

When AJ raised her head and turned toward him, the instrument panel lights revealed her bug-eyed stare. "Don't you mean who Sam's going to sleep with?"

"You don't understand, AJ. What Sam did to Radley is child's play compared to what she can do to a person while she's sleeping."

"She's sleeping like a serene little angel. Look at her."

"That all changes at about 2:00 a.m., when she turns crosswise. Her frog kick will send you onto the floor."

"Regardless, I'm not climbing into bed with someone I'm not married to, someone I only met five hours ago."

"AJ, we met on the phone eleven hours ago. But, you're right. I'll take the couch for the night."

When the pilot told them they would be landing in the Walmart parking lot in five minutes, the subject of who would be sleeping on the couch was still being debated.

Hunter dropped the couch conversation and moved to a more important issue. Could a person actually buy clothes at Walmart suitable for an appointment with the president?

They wouldn't have a minute to spare tomorrow, except while cruising at 30,000 feet. The answer had to be yes. Now to convince the doubter, AJ.

Except for two RVs at the far end of the parking lot, and some employees' vehicles along one side of the building, the main parking area was deserted at 11:05 p.m.

The chopper eased down onto the asphalt, sending swirling tornadoes of dust across the lot lit by the streetlights that lined its perimeter. Mercifully, the wop, wop ended, and the engine wound down to a stop.

Someone ran out of the store and stared at the helicopter sitting in the parking lot then hurried back inside.

"The place closes in fifty-five minutes. You two need to get your shopping done quickly," the pilot said. "Sam's zonked. We'll watch her."

The deputy, seated beside the pilot, pushed the door open.

Hunter and AJ slid out and strode toward the store's entrance.

"Wait for me!" Sam's shrill cry came from behind them.

The deputy lowered her to the ground.

Sam ran to meet them and reached for AJ's hand, not Hunter's.

If their quickly cobbled threesome for some reason didn't last, Sam's heart would be crushed. That was an unforeseen consideration quickly zooming to the top of his priority list.

Hunter had a possible solution, a risk-filled longshot. But he needed to pull the trigger on it before he lost the opportunity. And after tomorrow, all bets would be off, including longshots.

As Sam moved between them, stealing hands from both AJ and Hunter, he looked at AJ's smile.

Somehow, this had to work, or three hearts would be shattered, and Hunter Jones was not as resilient as Sam.

He had resigned himself to a life devoted to Sam only. Hunter wouldn't seek happiness for himself at Sam's expense. But would this be at Sam's expense? Only AJ could answer that question.

Thirty minutes later, AJ stood in front of a mirror outside the dressing room.

"A thirty-dollar, career-suiting blazer and a twenty-dollar, fold-over skirt to see the president? I'm going to look ridiculous."

"No you aren't. Besides we need to check out and get out of here before they close the registers and leave you with nothing."

She didn't look convinced.

"They match, AJ. They're both black. You look ... uh, rather bewitching."

"Bewitching? Maybe Bain and the Captain were right. I look like a witch. A dorky witch."

"No you don't," Sam said. "You look beautiful, just like Mom."

"Thanks, Sam." AJ whirled toward the dressing room. As she walked through the doorway, she swiped at her cheeks.

AJ was smitten. Sam was smitten with AJ. So was Hunter Jones.

Please, God, don't let me or anyone else mess this up.

At five minutes until midnight, Hunter directed the pilot to the open field by the road below his house, an area far removed from power lines.

With the chopper's light flooding the area and swirling clouds of dust fleeing the landing spot, the police helicopter touched down.

At straight up midnight, Hunter unlocked the door of his house and ushered AJ in. "Sam, show her where everything is in the house while I call Zach for a ride to the airport."

Hunter hit Zach's entry in his contacts and waited. On the third ring, he tried to recall if he had Medford Metro Taxicab in his contacts. It was beginning to sound like he would need to call them.

On the fifth ring, someone answered. "Hunter ..." Zach's voice was hoarse and his words sluggish. "... this had better be an emergency, or you might get unfriended."

"Unfriended? I feel so threatened."

"You don't want to be unfriended by a DJ, believe me. When they flame, the worm dieth not."

"Okay. I'm now threatened. But I need a ride to the airport at five o'clock in the morning."

"You mean you're too cheap to pay ten dollars a day for long-term parking but inconsiderate enough to wait until midnight to call me to bum a ride?"

Not a good start. "I don't have my truck, Zach. They kept—"

"Your truck never breaks down. You baby it like it was—uh, who's *they*?"

"The police are holding it for evidence. The crime scene crew was all over it last time I saw it."

"Crime scene? What's up, Hunter?"

"The Q-It CEO, Bratkowski, sent a team of ex-Spec Ops gunmen to kill me, Sam, and AJ, but we took *them* out instead. And we've got to be in DC for a meeting with President Gramm tomorrow after—"

"Hold it! Hold it. I thought you were a teetotaler. Did you fall off the wagon, or is this the result of binging on medicinal cannabis?"

"It's true, Zach. All of it, and that ain't even the half of it. You can probably listen to it on the news tomorrow. Just promise me you'll be at my place at 5:00 a.m. to get us to MFR for a six o'clock flight."

"Are you and Sam okay? And who is this AJ?"

"We're a little rattled, tired and I've got a splitting headache after the chopper ride."

"Chopper ride?"

"I told you that there was more to it."

"Who is AJ?"

"She's the Amazon who's sleeping over with me tonight. Wait. That didn't come out quite right."

"Do I need to call our accountability group at church? Sounds like you're really falling off the wagon, bro. And Amazon? You mean like Wonder Woman?"

"Wonder Woman? Zach, one look at her and you won't wonder if she's a woman. But that's another subject for another time. And, no, you don't need to call our accountability group."

"Does that mean I don't need to, or that you don't want me to."

"Just promise me you'll be here at five o'clock, and that you'll set your alarm *before* you fall asleep again."

"Sleep? How can I sleep after hearing your wild story and about your—do I need to pray for you, bro. Like right now?"

"Everything's fine. Set your alarm for 4:30 a.m. and get some sleep. See you at five."

"If you say so."

"Is that a yes?"

"I'll be there. I've gotta see this femme fatale who got to my best friend." Zach ended the call.

Hunter set his bedroom alarm for 4:30 a.m. then returned to the living room.

"Is everything okay, Hunter." AJ's low, sultry voice came over his right shoulder.

"It's fine. Zach's just being over-protective."

"Of who? Sam?"

"Of me. He's worried about you."

"What did you tell him, Hunter Jones?" AJ's hands went to her hips.

"I'm not sure. But he accused me of—never mind. We need to get some rest."

"I tucked Sam in and she was out before I could hit the light. I'm exhausted, but I need to wind down a little before I can sleep."

"Yeah. Me too." He took AJ's hand and led her to the couch.

She sat and patted the spot beside her.

Hunter plopped on the couch, feeling like he'd gained fifty pounds. Exhaustion had encroached and would soon take over his body and then his consciousness. But he had some questions for AJ before his mind went numb. She probably had some for him too.

"I heard you mention your accountability group. Is that a group at your church?"

"Yeah. But—"

"Why would your friend, Zach, think about—it was about me, wasn't it?"

"It was about my unfortunate use of the term sleepover."

"Look, Hunter Jones, I don't do things like this. Well, not under normal circumstances."

"Do you have a boyfriend, or anyone like—"

"No. I've never had a boyfriend, not really."

He was glad in one sense, sad in another. And then there were those words that had slipped out when they didn't know if they would be alive much longer. What had she said? *It never really matters with someone like me.*

She had sounded sad, maybe even lonely, when she uttered those words.

"When we were tied up in that clearing, wondering what would happen to us, what did you mean by relationships never really mattering to someone like you?"

She didn't reply.

"It's okay. You don't have to explain."

"Yes, I do." She paused for several seconds. "When my father was killed in the war, I was eleven. It made me an orphan and sent me into the foster care system. One family treated me like a daughter. Said they wanted to adopt me. That was my biggest dream of my young life, to be part of a family again, a real part, not a fake foster part. I was with them for nearly two years. But they were offered a job in another state, and I wasn't worth waiting for the adoption. They abandoned me, moved to Texas, and I got recycled in the system. There were four more homes in the next five years. I earned some scholarships and went off to college. Finally free from foster care."

As AJ told her story, her eyes took on a despairing look, haunting. The story had drained her usual vibrance.

"I can't imagine what you've been through. Sam lost her parents too. But at least she had someone. I'm not the greatest prize for a little girl, but I would never abandon her, and she knows that."

"Sam was more than lucky to have you. She was blessed. Anyone who watches the two of you would know that."

"Thanks. I try, but you never really know if you are enough, if you're doing—"

AJ muted his words with a finger over his lips. "You're more than enough for an orphaned girl like Sam. You're exactly what she needs."

"Today, you were exactly what I needed, when the Captain had gotten the drop on me. How did you get there so quickly and then take out a trained warfighter? What if …"

"What if I had failed? I didn't know if I would succeed or not. You know, I used to play women's fast pitch softball in high school, and I got a scholarship to play in college. I'm a good batter. When I ran toward you and the Captain, it was like hitting the ball hard and running full speed around the bases. When the ball doesn't clear the fence, you don't know how far you can go. You just run hard. I was headed for third as the fielder scooped up the ball. I could probably make third, but I needed to score to win the game."

"Aren't you supposed to look at the third base coach?"

"Yes. I did and it was Jesus. He said, 'All the way home, AJ.' So that's what I did. I went after the Captain with Bain's gun."

"And if you hadn't made it home?"

She sighed. "At least I'd know I did what I was supposed to do."

What did the wordsmiths call that? Uncommon valor? AJ was anything but common. "How did I ever find someone like you?"

* * *

When AJ laid against Hunter's shoulder, it seemed to be a perfect fit for her head. "Hunter, wasn't it more like I found you?"

"Yeah. I was looking for that Amazon that the service station attendant told me about, not Amazing Jane. Then you called me."

She'd told her story and didn't need to hear more about Hunter or Sam at this juncture. Fatigue would probably end their conversation soon, anyway.

AJ nestled into a comfortable position, a position made more comfortable and secure when Hunter's arm curled around her shoulders.

She didn't want to lose this feeling, or spoil it, or end it. Maybe just enjoy it for a while ...

The warmth and the gray fuzziness in AJ's mind had been invaded by rhythmical music with phrases about Christmas, about watching snow falling down and somebody begging someone not to go. She blinked the fuzziness away. That revealed an arm around her shoulders.

The arm refused to release her. And its owner's heavy breathing tickled her left ear.

A golden-haired princess had wedged herself between AJ and Hunter. All three had evidently been sleeping on his couch together.

If only every day of her life could start like this. But was it real? Was it more than just the aftermath of yesterday, more than simply the comradery of shared danger?

Hunter stirred and his eyes popped open. "AJ. What a pleasant surprise. But weren't you supposed to take the bed while I slept on the couch?"

"It seems that someone hooked their arm around me while we were talking last night, and they wouldn't let go."

"I can't blame them. You're a pretty good catch. The way Sam has her arms wrapped around your leg says she thinks so too."

"You two trapped me. I've been kidnapped."

"Kidnapped? I don't see any zip ties on you."

"They're invisible. That's the strongest kind. But, Hunter, sometime soon I need to know if you have any of those invisible ties on you."

Sam raised her head. "Mom, I—" She blinked her eyes twice. "AJ." Sam smiled. "I was dreaming, and I thought— never mind what I thought."

She turned her head toward Hunter. "When are you gonna take that Christmas thumb drive out of your alarm clock. We need *summer* music."

"I'll turn off the alarm. But we need to get a move on. Zach will be here in fifty-five minutes, then we've got a plane to catch."

Sam bounded toward her bedroom. "I'm gonna brush my teeth and get dressed."

Halfway to the door of her room, she whirled, ran back to AJ, and wrapped her arms around AJ's waist. "I love you, AJ." Then she was gone again.

The innocent confession of love from a child destroyed the lie that had plagued AJ from adolescence.

God had to love everyone. That was his nature. But Sam loved AJ simply for who she was. Maybe she was not some unlovable orphan to be discarded by everyone she met in life. At least not in Sam's eyes. But what about in Hunter's?

The room had become a blur as AJ's eyes welled.

Hunter stood studying her in that silent, awkward moment.

She couldn't read the expression on his face. She couldn't read anything at the moment. AJ tried to wipe away the tears but more took their place.

Everything had happened so quickly, too quickly. It couldn't be real and wouldn't last. But if she lost Sam and Hunter, AJ Scott didn't see a pathway forward in life. There would be nothing there for her.

Girl, you are psychotic. You're so tired of being alone that you'll grab anyone within reach and refuse to let go.

"AJ?" Hunter's voice.

She swiped at her cheeks and peered into Hunter's warm, blue eyes.

He laid a hand on her shoulder. "We've got as much or as little time as we need to sort all this out. But promise me you won't run away from it … from us. Sam couldn't survive losing you right now. You saw and heard what you've become to her."

She dipped her head slowly. "What about you?"

"After yesterday, I'd think that was obvious. I don't kiss a girl lightly."

"No. you do it rather vigorously. Where did you learn that? From listening to Smash Mouth?"

"That's not what I meant. I don't do it at all, unless I plan to marry that person. And I don't listen to punk rock."

"So you meant what you said yesterday, about spending life together?"

"AJ, I didn't know if we would live through the next few minutes, and I couldn't die without telling you how I felt."

"You actually cared about me, sight unseen? Guys don't do that, Hunter."

He cupped her cheek, "I was head-over-heels for you before I even saw you. Anybody who would take the risks you did for strangers, and would protect Sam with their own life, had to be someone special. And you even enjoyed the verbal sparring with me."

"It wasn't that I liked it. You attacked me and I defended myself. Besides, I had to make you understand that I'd never let anything happen to Sam. I was going to stick with her come what may."

Something moved near the front door.

AJ whirled and pressed against Hunter.

"Bro, you two don't look like you're ready to see the president."

Hunter drew a sharp breath. "Zach, what are you doing here?"

"You did call me, you know, about five hours ago and asked me to take you to the airport. I'm a bit early."

"How long have you been standing there?" Hunter's voice turned confrontational.

"Long enough. So this is AJ. You two were discussing some heavy-duty stuff, bro. But I can see why."

"For your information, we were discussing 'heavy-duty stuff' before we even saw each other." Why had AJ said that?

"So this was one of those Internet dating relationships?" Zach folded his arms and studied Hunter.

"No," Hunter said. "We played phone tag while we were running from some gunmen who were trying to kidnap Sam and kill me. AJ saved Sam and then she saved my life. That's all I need to tell you, dude."

"That's all you've got time to tell me. We've got to be out of here in thirty minutes if you're going to catch a six o'clock flight."

"AJ, get dressed and pile everything you're bringing on my bed. I've got a big duffle bag that all three of us can share. You take the master bath, and I'll take the other one. Whoever finishes first can help Sam pack her things."

"Twenty-nine minutes and counting, bro," Zach said. "You've got a continent to cross. Miss that flight and you're toast."

Chapter 27

"I want to see everything, but I can't see anything." Sam strained against her seat belt, trying to look out from her spot in the middle of the limo seat between Hunter and AJ. "What's that?" She pointed out AJ's window at a tall spire. "Wait, don't tell me. It's ... the Washington Moment."

"Washington Monument." AJ brushed a stray curly wisp from Sam's face.

The limo turned right at an intersection.

Sam pointed at the window. "But it's gone now."

"That's one excited young lady." The limo driver's eyes peered at AJ through the rearview mirror. "Other than the hair color, she looks just like her mother."

AJ glanced Hunter's way.

He smiled. "Could be."

Her face went hot. Probably glowing pink. "I—I'm actually not her mo—"

"But the job's still open and I've only interviewed one qualified applicant." Hunter's eyes held the teasing expression AJ had seen several times in the past twenty-four hours.

"Who was the applicant? The ever-present Ms. McCorkle?" AJ almost laughed at the contortions that name brought to Hunter's face.

"Yuck. Not her," Sam said.

The limo turned right again, and they were staring at—

"The White House!" Sam unlatched her seatbelt and stood.

A seatbelt alarm buzzed for a few seconds.

Hunter reached for Sam's shoulder.

"She's okay, Mr. Jones," the driver said. "I'll take it slow and easy until we stop by the West Wing."

Gardens, trees, a manicured lawn—a park-like setting stretched for hundreds of yards to their left.

The driver stopped the limo in front of the entrance to the West Wing. He unbuckled and twisted in his seat to face them. "Just show them the passes I gave you and your IDs. They'll take you to the Oval Office where the president is waiting for you."

AJ slid out of the limo.

Sam leaped out, looked up at the towering building to their left, and reached for AJ's hand.

Hunter circled the limo to AJ's side. "Come on. Let's do this."

"I don't know what to say to the president. Maybe I won't say anything. Then nothing stupid can slip out."

"I can talk to him for you, AJ." Sam beamed a smile up to her.

AJ returned it. "I'll bet you could talk to him for all three of us."

"You, young lady ..." Hunter said, "... will be on your best behavior and that means not talking over anyone. Okay?"

Sam nodded, but the impish expression on her face wasn't convincing.

Hunter took Sam's hand with his left, AJ's with his right, and all three headed toward the door leading them on what promised to be the last leg of this fantastic, frightening adventure.

A young man in a neat, freshly pressed uniform stood at the door and let them in.

After checking in with ROTUS, another man escorted them down a hallway and around a corner to the Oval Office door.

Inside the office, the president stood smiling in front of his desk near the Great U.S. Seal woven into the carpeting.

Hunter placed a hand on AJ's and Sam's backs and escorted them to President Gramm.

A person doesn't tromp on the Great U.S. Seal. AJ tried to step around the perimeter but when her foot nearly came down on some stars, she stumbled.

Hunter caught her arm and steadied her, preventing AJ from plowing into the president.

President Gramm responded with a warm smile. "My, what did I do to deserve the presence of these two lovely young ladies?" He gave Sam his hand.

"Hunter thinks we earned this vacation," Sam said as she shook the president's hand.

"It's good to meet you," he said, looking down at Sam. "I trust you had a good flight from the West Coast and hope you enjoy your earned vacation."

"The flight today was great. The flight yesterday was hair-raising," Hunter said. "And this is AJ Scott. She saved our lives."

President Gramm shook her hand. Then a look of concern creased his brow. "We heard your names on the news along with the mention of some shooting in Oregon. What happened yesterday?"

"If you haven't heard yet, you will shortly. We were pursued by hit men hired by James Bratkowski of Q-It."

"Bratkowski actually sent people to kill you?" The president's pleasant smile turned to a scowl.

"Yes. And to kill AJ and Sam too. AJ found Sam where I had hidden her in some bushes. I led them on a chase over the side of a mountain. When I came back, Sam was gone. Then this woman called me, and we played cell tag across Southern Oregon and into Eastern Oregon where we were eventually caught and interrogated. Then they planned to take us into the backcountry, kill us, and let the scavengers clean up their dirty work."

"My goodness. That settles it then."

"Settles what, sir?"

"I was debating whether you needed protection. When you go home, you're flying on a government plane with Secret Service protection until this episode with Q-It is laid to rest."

"Cool," Sam said.

"Is that really necessary?" It would be awkward, because AJ didn't have a home.

"Our national sovereignty and an election were just challenged by conspirators plotting treasonous treachery. Yes, it's only prudent to protect you. There may be those still at large who want to retaliate. We must ensure that they fail."

"I see your point, Mr. President. See what you get, AJ, for getting involved with me."

"I wouldn't change a thing, Hunter, except I would love to kick Mr. Bratkowski right in the—"

"That's enough, Amazon Jane."

"You said there would be no more name calling. Please forgive Hunter, Mr. President. It seems he can't help himself when he has an opportunity to annoy me."

The president chuckled. "Somehow, I don't think annoying you is foremost on his mind."

"Yeah." Sam looked up at President Gramm. "He even kissed AJ once."

"Only once?" The president grinned. "That's hard to believe."

"Well," Sam said. "Who knows what they did after I fell asleep last night."

AJ's cheeks burned.

The president cleared his throat. "If the skirmish has ended, Hunter, I need to hear more about what you planned to publish that would push Q-It to such extreme, criminal measures. We've been watching and waiting for someone to do the research you've done. Once we heard about your work and saw your credentials, I wanted to talk with you personally and privately, if that is even possible these days."

Hunter clamped a hand on Sam's shoulder. "Sam, the president needs to hear about my research, and we don't want to be interrupted while I tell him about—"

"About the carry insults?"

"The query results."

Sam glanced at Hunter then sidled up to AJ and gave her a look that begged for protection. "AJ and I will just listen while you talk about the big data stuff."

AJ gave Sam the shush signal.

"Sam is right, Mr. President," Hunter said. "Query results can *carry insults*, big time insults."

"Maybe I should be more careful about what I search for."

"Sir, it's not what you search for as much as it is what they decide to give you in return. You see, over time, the filtering and ordering of data returned by a search engine can change the thoughts and actions of people in social and political realms. It's possible to sway people in ways that determine the winner of any close election."

"How does that work? Most people have strong feelings about politics."

"It works by letting you think you're making up your own mind. Experiments have shown that when people are undecided about some issue, we can steer them to a desired conclusion by simply filtering and ordering the data that they ask for. We give them data that only leads to one conclusion, and that's the one they will draw."

"And Q-It's involved in this—swinging an election one way or the other simply by ordering and filtering data?"

"Yes. But Q-It will never admit that they're deliberately impacting elections. They would lose the public's trust and that would kill their business."

"And it could earn their management fines and prison sentences. But is it possible that this influence and the bias are accidental?"

"Not likely. Ninety-five percent of the IT industry sides with the political left. And their campaign contributions clearly reveal this."

"I need for you to explain to me how they sway people using Internet queries."

"How much time do you have, sir?"

"We have until dinnertime, about an hour and a half." "Okay. I'll give you the ninety-minute version." Hunter paused. "There are several ways to influence people using the data they have requested. Number one is manipulating the query results. My research shows that if query results are structured to favor one side of an issue, or one candidate for office, the majority of the voters who have not formed a strong opinion can be shifted to one side or the other based on the data they are given. You see, people trust search engines to be impartial, because they think it's just an algorithm doing the search."

"I thought it was programmed logic doing the search. You mean Q-It can change the *logic* anytime they want?"

"In effect, they can. It's done by putting their biasing parameters in a database that the query code reads and runs until the next time it synchs with the database. Q-It can turn a hard-left candidate into someone who looks acceptable to people who only vote for moderates. Many elections in America, including the presidency, are close. QIt can guarantee the winner in these elections. And I can predict the outcome, if no one intervenes in Q-It's little election-rigging scheme."

"And you're sure about that?"

"Positive. I've built a mathematical model. I ran it on the last election, one in which Q-It used their query scheme. It correctly predicted the winner of each gubernatorial and senatorial race that I analyzed. Then I ran my model on the last general election. It predicted your election by the slimmest of margins."

"Which is precisely what happened. What other techniques do they use?"

"You know that thing called auto completion? You start typing and they suggest completions?

"Yes. Sometimes it gets infuriating, because it changes what you typed to something else, something totally opposite of what you were typing. How can we stop these things?"

"The bottom line is, we need a monitoring system to detect biases when they are introduced."

"What if they won't let you monitor them?"

"That doesn't matter. We monitor them by running our own queries from our own computers using their search engine. To Q-It, it just looks like a lot of users doing searches."

"So they don't have to know they're being monitored?"

"No. But they could figure that out if they decided to analyze searches coming from our system's servers. I've spec'd out a monitoring system that can detect the use of these techniques early on. But we must be backed up by a fair-minded government in order to take action. If not, we've lost control of our elections."

"It sounds like we've also lost control of our nation. And once it's tilted too far in one direction, with nothing to stop the illegal election practices, the people will never get their nation back."

"Here's another thing Q-It does, Mr. President."

"Hunter, I'm losing track of all the ways these people cheat."

"But this one is even more insidious. If people are asking a question, programming bots provide programmed answers. You know, those little pull downs that appear at the top the query results page and provide canned answers to common questions. This technique works with text searches, with local queries, and even with voice-based assistants. Companies like Q-It love these bots because they take part of the load off Q-It's servers by reducing the total number of searches. And the programmed answers can shift opinion thirty percent more effectively than query results alone. I can tell you very accurately how many votes will be shifted to the left by these canned answers to common questions.

"Quite frankly, you're scaring me, Hunter. I'm not sure I want to hear those numbers."

"Then I'll move on. Another thing they can do is create stars. You know, the rock stars of politics. Q-It can shift traffic to give people positive publicity. Folks see the popularity rising and are quick to jump on the bandwagon and cheer their star into the White House. I've modeled the mathematics. If we detect it, I can predict how many votes star creation will shift."

"I'm getting a frightening picture. It's not only elections these people can impact. They could declare war on something or someone, or they could make a person appear worthy of a medal of honor. And, if they wanted to, they could make a fortune by manipulating stocks, and that's criminal."

"That's right, but here's another way to—"

"Another? You mean there's more?"

Yes. Here are two more ways Q-It commonly manipulates opinion. Obviously, they can censor you. Not let anyone see anything from or about you—well, nothing unless it's negative. And there are eight or nine ways Q-It can censor a person or an idea."

"They're circumventing the First Amendment and doing it on their own equipment while supposedly providing a free service. That raises some sticky legal questions. And whenever we've subpoenaed a big tech company, our investigation doesn't get very far, because they have all the data, and they only release what they want to."

"Finally, they—"

"Finally ... thank heaven," President Gramm said.

"That's probably not who they thank for those hellish censoring schemes. Finally, they can customize what they show you to *please* you, showing you only what they think you want to see based on your search history. And you keep clicking on their links and feeding your unsuspecting, selfish mind a lot of opinion-altering information mixed in with ego satisfaction."

The president sat up in his chair. "But we're talking about more than an election here."

"Yes, sir. We're talking about liberty in America. Or the loss of it. These IT giants can shape our world into a brave new world, or something even worse, something Orwellian.

"I knew some of this was happening, but I had no clue how impactful it was. I want to stop this IT power grab. It's insidious, almost demonic. How do we stop it?"

"First, we should build a monitoring system that can detect these manipulations as soon as they're activated. Second, we can expose them. Let all the people know what we've detected, what it's doing, and what it is capable of doing. Show the people how they're being duped by IT predators who think our citizens are stupid. That'll really tick them off. Ticked off consumers make a lot of noise. We also need to take away the free pass we've given to the IT giants—we don't give a free pass to the media—and then we must pass laws to prosecute the violators."

"But is that enough to convince the people and a more difficult audience, Congress, that we need legislation?"

"My third proposal should help. We will build a model to predict the impact of the violations. Then we make public our predictions in advance of the next election, and we include all the supporting evidence. When they see what's about to happen, it will cause some people to change their minds about erroneous ideas that influenced them. It will probably cause quite a few to swing back to their original thoughts on issues and candidates."

"It still could be a hard sell to the good old boys and gals in the Senate."

"That's why we need one more thing. We need evangelists in government, the media and the culture, people who can convince America what's at stake. Otherwise, we could reach the point of no return before we realize it. And, as you said, the America we know and love would be lost and unrecoverable."

AJ was shocked as Hunter had piled crime upon crime that Q-It had been inflicting on an unsuspecting populace. "Hunter," she put her hand on his shoulder. "I knew your work was important, but I had no idea how important."

Hunter nodded. "Now you see what was at stake and why Q-It wanted to eliminate me before my research results were published. And I had lined up some influential people and organizations to distribute my report."

"And I walked right into Q-It's crosshairs."

"I'm glad you did, AJ. Well, after the fact, I'm glad."

The president leaned forward and pounded a fist on the coffee table. "I want this stopped! This is far more than a traditional, political battle for the minds of Americans. This is a battle for the soul of America. I thank you, three brave souls, for not yielding to the wrong that's warping the truth and for risking your lives. And thank you, Hunter, for putting numbers and actual impacts to what we only suspected but now can know."

"Thank you, Mr. President, for bringing us here and being willing to listen to my boring details about a seditious search engine."

"Seditious. That's in interesting way to describe it. May I borrow those words, Hunter?"

"I'd be honored. But I don't think Q-It will."

President Gramm chuckled. "Changing the subject ... if you're agreeable, I made arrangements for the three of you to have dinner at the White House and spend the night. I didn't know about Ms. Scott at the time, so I only planned for two bedrooms, but we've got a lot more—"

"How many do you have?" Sam said.

"Well the White House has one-hundred thirty-two rooms, more than thirty bathrooms. It has six levels, so we have three elevators and eight staircases. And, goodness, there are over four-hundred doors, enough get to lost in the residence."

Sam's mouth opened wide, and she mouthed a silent "Wow."

"Two bedrooms will work just fine, Mr. President," Hunter said.

Sam's smile spread the width her face. "I get to sleep with you, AJ."

"I can't believe this." AJ shook her head and one eye overflowed.

Hunter took her hand. "What's wrong?"

"No one would believe this." She looked at President Gramm. "Especially you, Mr. President."

"We might if you'd tell us," Sam said.

"When I left my apartment yesterday, everything I owned was in my Jeep Cherokee. I found out a few minutes later that my job had just gone up in legal smoke and red tape, because the county shut down our espresso stand. At that moment, I was homeless, jobless, and wondering where I would spend the next several nights. And look where I am."

President Graham laughed softly. "He's a good God, isn't He?"

AJ nodded and wiped a tear from her cheek.

"And he is a *just* God," Hunter said. "He says that he repays affliction with affliction and shows no partiality when he does it. Wrongdoers, such as Q-It, will be paid back."

AJ's gaze went from Hunter to the president. "What do you suppose the law will do to the instigators at Q-It?"

Sam's mischievous smile spread across her face. "I've got subjections. Make the other engines put bad stuff in the carry results for that rat Kowski."

"You mean you've got suggestions for the query results for Bratkowski?"

"Whatever."

AJ took Sam's chin and turned her head toward AJ. "But, Sam, God says vengeance belongs to Him not to us."

Sam grinned. "We belong to Him too. So why can't we be part of the vicious?"

"You mean the vengeance."

"Whatever."

Chapter 28

Jim Bratkowski hit the Captain's secure-cell contacts entry, then stopped before pressing the call icon.

It was now 6:00 p.m., and it had been nearly twenty-four hours since Jim had given the authorization to dispense with the three troublemakers. Hearing no news for a day meant something hadn't gone according to plan.

But what if the worst happened, and the Captain was dead? What if someone else had his phone? Calling could incriminate Jim.

He cancelled out of the phone call.

A knock sounded on his office door.

"Jim, it's Andy."

"Come in." If Jim was agitated by the lack of communication, Andy was probably manic.

Andy hurried to the chair across the desk from Jim. "I just did a search for Hunter Jones and couldn't find anything online. Have you heard from the Captain?"

"Think about it, Andy. That's your search algorithm at work. What did you expect? You blacklisted Jones. Have you tried national news?"

"No."

"Because that's where you'll see Jones mentioned if he makes the news." Jim opened his browser and searched for the Oregon-based, conservative news commentator he seldom listened to, one who covered important events in his home state.

One link returned in the query results knotted his stomach. The linked article was titled, Data Guru and His Accomplice Thwart Attempt on Their Lives.

"Take a look at this Andy. This is our worst-case scenario. It says Jones, his little girl, and a woman who was with them are all unharmed."

Andy moved behind Jim and read the screen. "It all took place yesterday evening. It looks like Jones killed the Captain and seriously injured his other two men. And he flew to DC this morning. If Jones can connect those men to us, we're in deep trouble."

"I almost dialed the Captain before you came in. The police might have somebody monitoring that phone. I would have incriminated myself."

"How much do you think Jones knows?"

"Too much. He knows we are his biggest threat, and he's probably figured out that the Captain and his team were mercenaries. We will be suspects. And we could be getting a visit from the police any time now. The only reason we haven't may be because they have the cell and are hoping we will call."

"Jim, the last call the Captain made was to my cell phone. Whoever has the phone can look in the log and see that. We've got to do something now, or this will blow up in our faces."

"Correction. *You* have to do something, Andy. It's your biased search algorithm that Hunter Jones was going to expose. *You* are responsible for running it, and *you* received that final call from the hired assassin."

"So you're throwing me under the bus? I should have seen this coming a year ago when we agreed to keep this a secret project."

"You can do what I'm planning on doing, hiding behind the Communications Decency Act."

"You mean that section that says we're not actually content providers, therefore we can't be prosecuted like those who publish?"

"Exactly."

"Jim, this isn't a case of us not being punishable for what our users do. It's about us being a different kind of publisher. We republish selected content on demand. And we often censor what we republish. We give service to one publisher, then deny it to another."

"But that can't be proven." At least Jim still believed it couldn't, because all of the big IT corporations practically required a blood oath of loyalty before anyone could peek behind the curtain and see the inner workings of the most influential software code in the world. But what if another Hunter Jones came along and—

"Are you listening?" Andy paused. "Section 230 of the Communications Decency Act was designed to promote an open Internet. But our algorithm does just the opposite. It's partially closing the Internet. I don't think we can legally hide behind this act."

"I'm sorry that you and your algorithm can't hide behind Section 230."

"What do you mean by *my* algorithm? If I can't hide neither can you."

"But, Andy, I'm one step removed from what you're doing. I don't even know the details of your algorithm. It's yours, and my lawyer will make sure the buck stops at your desk. I might get fined, but I get to keep wearing my street clothes and—"

"You can't do that, Jim. You wouldn't do—"

"But I can and I will. And I certainly didn't know enough to have conspired to commit murder. Only you could have done that. If you'll remember, the original call to the Captain was placed on *your* phone."

"So that's the way it's going to be? You're one of the richest people in the world, and I'm your fall guy for kidnapping, attempted murder, which were entirely *your* ideas?"

"Sorry, Andy. I've got too much invested."

"So that's your final—"

"Yes. That's the way it has to be."

"You really should have taken more interest in my algorithms, Jim."

"No. I needed to keep a proper distance from them in case something like this happened."

"But some of my code didn't keep a proper distance from you."

"Don't try playing games with me. I've already made my decision regarding the Hunter Jones issues."

"Your decisions have all been documented from multiple sources, including recordings from your digital assistant."

"But I killed my assistant weeks ago and you don't use yours."

"And I resurrected yours several days ago and a modified version of mine three days ago."

"I don't believe you. You're bluffing."

"Try me, Jim. I can give you the proof now, or you can wait until you hear it played in Federal Court."

"You are a double-crossing, little—"

"Funny. I remember calling you that a few minutes ago. So, who's your fall guy now, Mr. B?"

Chapter 29

As incredible as the night at the White House had been, the flight home in the Gulfstream, escorted by three Secret Service agents, was even more impressive to AJ. The seats were better than first class, and they were allowed to help themselves to any food or beverages stocked on the plane.

At 9:30 a.m. local time, the jet touched down at the Medford airport under pale blue summer skies.

Two vans with dark windows waited for them at the curb near the baggage claim area.

Fifteen minutes later, their van stopped in the driveway of Hunter's house.

The modest-size house on the hillside looked like a home should look, serene on a summer morning.

Ahead of them, parked side-by-side in a wide spot in the circle drive, sat her Jeep and Hunter's pickup.

Hunter stepped out of the van and pointed at his truck. "The Deschutes County Sheriff was good for his word."

Agent Jacobs nudged Hunter toward the front door of the house. "Let's not dilly dally. We need to keep you three out of sight until we know the area is secure."

The first thing that caught AJ's attention after entering the house was the blinking red light on the living room phone.

Jacobs stopped AJ, Sam, and Hunter near the front door while the agent checked the house. After a couple of minutes, he emerged from the kitchen. "The house is secure."

"My clothes are packed up in my Jeep. When can I bring some of them in?"

"Later," Jacobs said. "Give us an hour or so to check things out."

"Why don't you help Sam unpack, AJ while I check the phone messages."

Sam hooked AJ's arm and pulled her toward Sam's bedroom. "Dump it all on my bed."

"But Hunter's things are in the duffle bag too."

"It's okay, AJ. I've seen his gross underwear before. You should see them after he works out at the gym. I almost puked when—"

"I've got the picture." But it still seemed like she was intruding. After two days, the feeling persisted that, though she was in a wonderful setting with people she ached to belong with, AJ Scott still remained outside a glass barrier. She could look in but wasn't actually with them.

Hunter entered Sam's room and stopped inside the doorway. "The first message was from the Deschutes County Sheriff saying that our vehicles are parked in the driveway and the keys are on the kitchen counter. He said not to ask how the keys got into the house. The second was from Zach, wondering if we made it back safe and sound. I'll call him in a bit. I've got an idea that I think Zach is going to love."

The smirky smile on his face got her attention. "Are Sam and I going to love this idea?"

"Sam will. Fame is a fleeting thing. We've got to capitalize on our celebrity status while we can."

"Celebrity status? I feel more like a victim."

Hunter laughed. "AJ, you don't make a very good victim. You're the kind of victim who eliminates the perpetrators or drives them crazy like you did to me." His voice had softened on the last phrase.

"So you're a perpetrator?"

172

Hunter didn't reply.

But what he'd just said might be the set up for what was coming, the talk about *them*. They couldn't put it off much longer. And with them settling into a sort of protective custody at Hunter's house, the talk would likely take place in the next few hours ... or perhaps minutes.

"I should call Zach now." Hunter headed toward the living room.

Sam had dumped out the clothes on her bed.

"Come on, Sam. Let's put some of these in the wash."

Ten minutes later, AJ stood in the utility room listening to the washing machine sloshing clothes while she looked out the window at her Jeep filled with her clothes and whatever else AJ Scott owned in this world. She needed to unpack a few things from the Jeep just to have something to wear.

Hunter appeared in the doorway.

Sam followed Hunter and stopped beside him.

"Guess what?" Hunter said. "We're doing our own version of Good Morning America tomorrow." He hooked his thumbs in his shorts pockets and waited.

"Good Morning America? What's that supposed to mean?"

"I gave Zach the nutshell version of what I told President Gramm and asked if his boss would like to do a whole program that broke my story."

"Were they interested?"

"Zach went ballistic, in a good way. Susan was salivating the moment she heard the idea. They're lining up network radio and TV. It'll all be live from the radio station, which backs to their Medford TV station."

"Is this really that interesting to—"

"AJ, this is a big story that impacts all Americans. You said, yourself, that you didn't realize how important my findings were. The only hang up is that the Secret Service men want to make sure the area is secure, especially if we end up outside and start drawing a crowd."

"A crowd? I'm not sure about this, Hunter. What do I have to do?"

"We're going casual. Just wear something summery, like the shorts and tank top you wore when you came to the park."

"And what else?"

He pulled her toward the living room.

"Just be your beautiful self. Answer any questions addressed to you, but you don't have to prepare anything. We want this to be natural. We're just ordinary, true blue Americans talking about what happened to us. I'll work on a speech to motivate the crowd after I tell them how they've been deceived. How does that sound?"

"Okay, as long as I don't have to give a speech."

"You don't, but I need to go work on mine for a bit. Make a few notes. This needs to punch Americans in the gut, and it's the kind of thing that needs to come from the heart more than the head. It shouldn't take me long to prepare. Then … you and I need to talk." Hunter stopped and sat on the couch.

AJ sat beside him.

"We do need to talk. You and I have flown by all the usual things people talk about. We've been going at a breakneck speed for two days. We ran a lot of stop lights."

"But we accomplished a lot in those two days, didn't we?" His bright blue eyes met her gaze and he waited.

A knock sounded on the front door.

"I guess what we accomplished in the last two days will have to wait." Hunter stood.

AJ stood and looked out the window beside the front door.

Two men in suits waited on the front porch.

One of the Secret Service agents stood beside them.

Hunter reached the door first and opened it.

Agent Jacobs motioned toward the two men. "The DOJ has gotten involved in this case. We have two FBI agents who would like to ask you some questions."

Hunter nodded and the tallest FBI agent reached out a hand. "I'm Special Agent Peterson."

Hunter shook Peterson's hand.

"And this is Special Agent McCheney. We have some questions regarding your knowledge of who authorized the attempts on your life."

"Do you mean the attempts on the lives of AJ Scott, Samantha Wilson, and myself?" He put a hand on AJ's shoulder and looked down at Sam who had moved to his side.

"Yes. For all three of you. And thanks for clarifying."

AJ motioned toward the couch. "Please, have a seat, gentlemen."

She had just played the role of hostess like this was her house. Something seemed to be changing. But was it real or imagined?

After the men sat, AJ took the easy chair.

Sam plopped down in her lap and studied the two men.

Hunter brought in a chair from the dining room and sat beside AJ. "You're looking at the three people Bratkowski wanted to have killed."

"That's what we wanted to talk to you about, Mr. Jones," Peterson said.

"I should hope so," Sam huffed. "People like that rat Kowski can't just go around shooting people."

McCheney faked a cough, but the laugh beat out the cough and produced something between a horse's whinny and sounds that come from the other end.

"Did you hear that?" Sam pointed at McCheney. "It sounded just like—"

AJ cupped Sam's chin and turned her head until their gazes locked. "That's enough, drama princess. Let these men ask their questions."

"If you had a gun pointed at your head, maybe you'd be dramatic too."

"Sam, I had one jammed into my back, several times."

"But they didn't make it do that click, click thing like they were gonna shoot you."

"Enough, Sam." Hunter's voice closed Sam's mouth. "Agent Peterson, I assume you were about to ask how we knew Bratkowski was involved."

"That's where we were headed. Did you hear him mentioned at any time while they held you?"

"Yes," Hunter said. "One of the men said his name when talking about the man who had hired them, the one giving the orders. He acted like it was a slip of the tongue, but one of the other men said it didn't matter. The implication was that they were about to kill us."

"I heard Bratkowski's name too," AJ said.

"Yeah," Sam said. "Somebody needs to put a gun against his head and make it go click, click. I bet he'd have to go tee tee too."

Peterson chuckled then covered his mouth.

Sam turned and looked at AJ then scanned each face in the room. "Well, I was just telling the truth. You're not supposed to lie to the FBI."

Peterson wrote something down on his notepad. "I take it that all three of you heard Bratkowski mentioned as the instigator."

"We all heard it," Hunter said.

Peterson scrawled some more notes then looked up at Hunter. "What other evidence do you have that suggested Bratkowski was involved?"

"Not even twenty-four hours after my interview went viral on YouTube, two gunmen tried to capture Sam and me in Shady Cove. I had become a personal threat to Mr. Bratkowski. My research report, soon to be released, would threaten his primary business, Q-It Incorporated."

"Do you know anything else that implicates Bratkowski?"

Hunter nodded. "Three men held us. The big dude they called the Captain acted like it was time to shoot us, but he also acted like he needed permission. He couldn't use his cell phone where they were holding us. There was no cell service. So he drove back toward the main campground at Paulina Lake to place a call. That was about eight o'clock in the evening, maybe eight thirty. If you check the calls on his cell, I'll bet you find a call to James Bratkowski."

Peterson took some more notes. "If this goes to trial, can we count on you to testify in Federal Court?"

"You bet we'll testify," Hunter said.

"I can swear to tell the truth too. Can I testify?" Sam said.

"If we need you, you can." McCheney winked at AJ.

Sam pointed at McCheney. "You're flirting with AJ. You better not do that She only kisses Hunter."

"Sam." AJ took Sam's shoulders and spun her around. "The drama is over. You can go to your room until—"

Peterson cleared his throat, "Actually, we're all through here. And, just so you can rest a little easier, James Bratkowski and a vice president at Q-It, Andrew Rosenburg, are in custody in Seattle. We're just firming up some evidence before charges are filed. I'm not the prosecutor, but I know the woman who is. I don't think you have any more to fear from anyone at Q-It."

Peterson and McCheney stood.

"I hope they throw'em into prison and lock away the key," Sam said.

"You mean throw away the key," AJ said.

"Whatever."

"What about the two gunmen who survived?" Hunter said.

"One has a severe concussion. We don't know what kind of shape he'll be in when he gets over it. Somebody cracked his skull, literally."

"It was AJ," Sam said. "She can hit home runs even when the baseball is as big as a head."

"Continuing ..." Peterson said. "The one who was shot is cooperating with us. Like I said. You are probably safe now."

There were no more questions and the two FBI agents left.

Knowing that the danger had ended was comforting, and it appeared that justice would be served on the perpetrators at Q-It.

The next item of business, the issue of AJ and Hunter, both excited and frightened AJ. Her life had reached this point before. Happiness had teetered in front of her, almost within reach. This is where it had always fallen apart.

Sam had retreated to her bedroom, leaving AJ and Hunter alone.

AJ sat down on the couch and patted a spot beside her.

"About those accomplishments ..." He sat down beside her. "If you'll remember, I've already proposed to you."

"No, Hunter. You said you'd like to spend time with me on planet Earth. Nobody has ever thought I was worth being part of their family. Why should I believe you would be any different?"

"Your mom and dad thought you were worth it."

"Because they had to. I was born to them. I was theirs."

"Then just promise me you'll be mine. But there will be a few differences. It won't be like living with your parents."

"Differences? Like what?"

"You'll wear my ring and all that goes along with that."

"What do you mean by all that goes along with that?"

"Doggone it, AJ. Do I have to spell it out? I love you. I have since our third or fourth phone call."

"How could you know that even before seeing me?"

"You were risking your life for Sam and she was getting pretty chummy with you. Then when we met after those phone calls, I knew my heart had made the right call."

"Impressive. That's the longest speech I've heard you give about matters of the heart. But you don't actually know that much about me. So how can—"

"I know all I need to know. You're a beautiful person, inside and out. You love Sam and you've risked your life more than once while saving Sam's life and mine. We share the same faith, both Jesus followers. Come on, AJ, it doesn't get any more perfect than that."

"Don't you want to know anything else?"

"I don't think so. What?"

"I told you he was clueless." Sam's voice came from behind them. "Tell him, AJ. He'll never ask."

"I love you too, Hunter. I began to love the person Sam described to me even while we bickered over the phone. I didn't realize how strong love is until I had to—you know. Then when I woke up with you and Sam wrapped around me ..." Tears began to flow, and they wouldn't stop.

For more than ten years, AJ believed life had taught her that she was a person who was broken in a way that meant no one could love her. Then Sam and Hunter had broken through her defenses and penetrated to her heart. And the way they had met, only a sovereign God could have orchestrated all of that, including bringing them out alive.

And God's purposes transcended making them a family. He had saved Hunter's research which would stop one of the most serious and insidious threats to America since its founding,

AJ Scott shouldn't be crying. She should be laughing and celebrating. AJ wiped her cheeks.

Hunter's arms pulled her in. "Like President Gramm said, 'He's a good God', isn't He?"

She looked up into his blue eyes and nodded.

Hunter evidently took that as an invitation, and he kissed her.

Sam bounced on the floor, clapping. "I knew it. I knew it."

When he released AJ, she leaned down eye-to-eye with Sam. "Did you know it even when the gunmen sent me to get Hunter and you started yelling that you—"

Sam clamped a hand over AJ's mouth. "Don't say it. When I get mad, sometimes I get mellow and dramatic."

"Do you mean melodramatic?"

"Whatever. But, uh … when we met, remember I told you I was a handful?"

"I remember."

"Well, Hunter says there's always a lot of drama when I'm around. I guess you'll have to get used to that."

"I love you, Sam. As long as you don't ever forget that, I can put up with a little drama."

"Uh, AJ … it's more like a lot. When I'm around, stuff happens."

Chapter 30

Though Hunter willed it to slow, the presto tempo in his chest would not relent. He breathed in deeply, blew it out slowly, and plopped into a chair in the studio. It was the same chair he had sat in when this adventure started five days earlier. Nearly a lifetime ago.

"We go live in twenty minutes," Zach said. "Are you ready for this?" He shifted in his chair and moved closer to the sound controls.

"I'm a little nervous, because the audience is a lot bigger than last time. But I've got some notes to use if I need a crutch." He shook his head. "That's an understatement. I don't need a crutch. I need a pacemaker."

Zach patted his shoulder. "Then let's talk about something else. You know, to keep your mind off your impending heart attack." He paused. "How did your sleepover go?"

"Quit calling it a sleepover. We were chaperoned by three Secret Service agents. They took over and turned my place into a safe house."

The door to the studio opened. Sam and AJ stepped inside.

Zach looked up at the two women. "Hi, Sam. Hello, AJ— uh, what happened to your eye?"

Hunter had watched AJ try her best to cover it with makeup this morning. But his nosey friend, Zach, would never miss an opportunity to investigate a shiner like the one tainting AJ's beautiful face.

Zach gave him his bug-eyed stare. "Bro, tell me you didn't hit her."

"Nobody hit me, Zach," AJ said.

"Yeah. That's what all the abused spouses say. You ran into a door, right?"

"She's not a spouse and she hasn't been abused. I tried to warn her, dude. But she wouldn't listen."

"Let me get this straight, bro. You lost your temper, warned her, and then clobbered her?"

"Hardly. I warned her about two hours before Sam kicked her in the face," Hunter said.

Zach's eyes widened with recognition. "I thought you were smarter than that, bro. You let your girlfriend sleep with Sam? That's grounds for a breakup or a divorce."

"I'm sorry, AJ," Sam said. "I was dreaming and I just sorta' kicked."

"I would have been fine if you hadn't been crosswise in the bed."

"Or if her feet were pointed the other way," Hunter said.

The studio phone played a strange digital ditty.

"Hang on everybody." Zach answered. "Okay ... got it." He hung up. "There's a crowd outside and its growing. People are mobbing the place. They've surrounded all the TV crews."

"What kind of billing did Susan give me? Hunter Jones, conspiracy theorist and data geek?"

"Nothing out of the ordinary. You know, Hunter Jones eliminates a team of assassins and saves America."

"Zach, that's not—"

"Bro, chill out. She knows how to create headlines that are sensational but sane. Just so you know, you're supposed to give your speech in here then move outside for the press conference with the media. And we'll try to get some interaction with the audience."

Zach waved Sam and AJ toward the door. "Time for you two to go to the lobby. The interview will be on the PA system, so you can listen until we all move outside together."

Before AJ cleared the doorway, she turned to Hunter. "Kathy just called. She turned the tables on those county bureaucrats."

"Did she reopen her espresso shop?"

"Yes. She modified the inside so she can serve coffee from windows on both sides. That makes room for two more cars. She can queue up eleven cars instead of nine. I've got my job back."

"That's good news, if you still want the job."

"And why wouldn't I?" AJ's forehead wrinkled, but it wasn't her cute, contrived frown.

"The day's not over, AJ. A lot can happen in a day."

"What's that supposed to mean? I don't intend to go on welfare, you know."

"We can talk about it later."

"You'll have to remind him," Sam said. "When he gets busy, he always forgets stuff."

"Not this time, Sam," Hunter winked at her. It sent Sam into a mouth-opened, eyes-wide look of delight.

When the door closed behind AJ and Sam, Zach studied Hunter's face for a few seconds. "Bro, I've gotta know this. You've been with her nearly every waking moment for almost three days. What's she like?"

After falling asleep on the couch, Hunter had been with AJ for more than their waking moments, but this was not the time to raise such issues with an overzealous accountability partner. "She's a believer. A strong Jesus follower, and she's like nobody I've ever known before."

"You can say that again. She's ... she's gorgeous. Well, except for that ugly shiner."

"And AJ swings a mean bat. She cracked the skull of one of the gunmen."

"I get it. She's one of those slender types, with a sweet swing, who can knock it out of the park."

"Yep. That's AJ. And she and Sam are inseparable."

"I know it's early, but with all that going for you two, have you popped the question?"

Hunter didn't reply.

"Then have you approached the question?"

"Sort of."

"Come on, bro. I was the one we agreed would probably get married first. You said you *never* would. But it sounds like she already took you over the fence with her sweet swing."

"There's nothing for her to hit yet, Zach. I haven't actually served her that fat pitch."

"Dude, don't let the shot clock expire. You need to—"

"You really like to mix your metaphors. Do all DJs to that?"

A red light on the wall flashed several times.

"Later, dude. We're on in sixty seconds." Zach adjusted Hunter's mic and slid some levers on the mixing console. "Okay, we're on in 5, 4, 3, 2, 1, welcome to Zach's Facts, folks, and have we got a show for you."

After the brief introduction Hunter needed to hook his audience if he expected them to stick with him through the driest part of his speech, the data-related information. He started by recounting their hair-raising adventure up to the point where the three gunmen were preparing to shoot him, AJ and Sam.

He left his audience hanging in suspense, a perfect time to explain why he, Sam and AJ were captured to be interrogated and murdered.

"The people allegedly behind this murder attempt manage the operations of Q-It. They had made plans to subtly and seditiously seize control of political power in America and to never let go."

Hunter paused to let his statement sink in.

Zach mouthed. "Dead airtime. Not good."

Hunter continued. "So how can a company like Q-It seize control? They first would have to influence all of you, the American people. Though you may not realize it, they do that in several ways each time you use their search engine."

"Q-It has eight ways of manipulating the information they provide you to make you believe you're drawing your own conclusions while they lead you to the conclusion they've made for you."

Hunter quickly iterated through the methods of swaying users that he had explained to President Gramm. "Keep in mind that they've been improving their methods for nearly three years. But with only a few months experience under their belt, they came within a whisker of stealing the last presidential election. That paints a big question mark on the next election."

He paused, shorter this time. "We live in a nation where executives of the IT giants wield more power than politicians. The IT giants are all aligned politically with the far left. Some with the radical left. With America evenly divided between the two opposing sides, Q-It, using their search engine, can now swing an election their way, to the left, every time.

"You might ask what's wrong with that? There's no way to whitewash the answer. The driving force behind the left's agenda is evil and it's damaging. It's a radical political orthodoxy that is anti-God, anti-freedom, anti-you and anti-me.

"This agenda benefits the supposed *elitists* who have absolutely no understanding of the reality of the human condition, and who are incapable of saving this sin-cursed world. In their arrogance, they'll promise to save the world socially, environmentally, morally and politically and give you economic justice in the process. But all they can deliver is deception and a society that will degenerate to moral bankruptcy with Big Brother in control.

"For three years, Q-It has been quietly and persistently teaching you their way of looking at society's problems. Consciously, and with malevolent intent, they have influenced you, hoping you wouldn't discover what they were doing. How does it make you feel being manipulated as if you were a gullible child who doesn't know what's best for them? It raises my temperature to about two-hundred and twelve degrees.

"You, the American people, want fairness. But it's not what you're getting. The left, aided by their media lackeys and corporations like Q-It, have overplayed their hand by spreading lies and suppressing the truth. Anyone who disagrees with their imposed consensus is called a racist, a dunce, or insane. And Q-It's query results slant everything to agree with that consensus.

"When I look at Q-It, I think about HAL in *2001 A Space Odyssey*. If we were to let them continue, one day we would realize what they're doing, and we would tell them to relinquish their power. And, like HAL, they would say, 'Sorry, can't do that.' We would ask, 'Can't or won't?' And we would get no reply. At that moment, we would realize that it was too late. But right now, it's not too late."

"Where are we being taken by out-of-control IT corporations? Regardless of what some may think, it's not to a brave new world. It's to a world that's becoming Orwellian, a world increasingly invaded by greedy power seekers who, by appearing helpful, want to force us to live life and see life their way in every way, from the ballot box to the bedroom.

"In light of this, what must we do now? First, we demand that they give us the truth. Real Americans are tough. We can take the truth, whatever it is. But we want our decisions made based on reality not Q-It's venality.

"Next, the criminals in that corporation must be held to account. We cannot let them slide by without prosecution. To do so would bring the end of the rule of law. And that's the end of America. It would also be the beginning of a nightmare, because the most powerful nation on earth would have become lawless.

"How did our government let this happen? Historically, if a media company got too big for its britches, the government split them up to break the monopoly and foster healthy competition.

"However, the IT giants, like Q-It, have gotten preferential treatment, a special deal. The federal government does not hold them liable for bullying, or other tyrannical behavior, like the government does the media outlets. Why were they allowed to skate by? Because these IT corporations promised to be neutral platforms, serving the American people, allowing us to freely exchange information and ideas.

"But in their arrogance, these privileged elitists began to discriminate against all people, religions, and ideologies with which they disagreed. If they don't like you or your ideas, they steal your voice—often without you even knowing it—and they foster another voice that ridicules and criticizes you." He paused. "This must be stopped."

"Even if we are able to fix this enormous problem, there is a mess, the pollution Q-It created. If someone creates toxic waste in the physical environment and people get sick or die, the perpetrators get punished and they have to clean it up. Sometimes people go to prison. But what happens if somebody or some organization does the equivalent in the cyber environment? How do you clean up messed up minds?"

Hunter paused briefly.

"We do not have laws adequate for managing this type of invasion into the lives of Americans. The Sherman Antitrust Act, maybe—if we would invoke it.

"One thing that must be cleaned up is Q-It's version of leftist ideology. It never asks what it can do for its country. It only asks what it can *impose on* its country.

"Our nation's history means nothing to them. Or should I say, they want history to mean nothing, because they don't want to be bound by it or to owe it anything. That includes the heroes and heroines who secured our history by their blood, sweat, tears and ingenuity.

"The past is an obstacle that must be removed, so they tear down our monuments and demonize the monumental people that we have historically honored. And then they honor what is shameful.

"This kind of behavior isn't new in human history. As the Apostle said almost 2,000 years ago, 'their end is their own destruction, their god is their stomach, and they glory in their own shame.'

"And the media is complicit. Journalists, you bear guilt here. Why? Because it is not your job to be the mother bird, regurgitating predigested information to cram down the throats of the American people. Your job is to tell us what happened while our own intellect informs us of its significance. But you cannot, because you don't know what is truly significant. Worst of all, you indoctrinate our young people with a venomous worldview.

"Now that is a bleak portrait of where we are and the direction we are headed. But, fellow Americans, it is not where we *have* to be. It is not where we *should* be. And, by God's grace it is not where we *will* be.

"Are you ready to reclaim this nation?"

"Uh, Hunter?"

"I said, are you—"

"Hunter?" Zach laid a hand on his shoulder.

Hunter covered his mic. "Yeah."

"There are several thousand people outside of the station. Young people, old people, kids. More are pouring in."

"I'm busy Zach. Tell them to go away."

"But it's *you* they want to hear from. They want to see you, AJ, and Sam."

"You sure about that?"

"Yes. The Secret Service agents are out there. They don't look happy, but they are scouring the area to keep it safe for you. Here's a mic you can carry with you to continue, but please continue outside. We've turned on our external speakers so they can hear you." Zach handed Hunter the portable mic and covered it with Hunter's hand. "As soon as you're ready, uncover your mic and, for heaven's sake, keep talking. Let's go."

Hunter took his hand off the mic. "I said, are you ready to reclaim America as the land of the free, free from tyranny of any kind?"

As Hunter carried his mic through the lobby, he took AJ's hand. She pulled Sam with her.

"Come on, you two." Hunter walked out the door into the warm morning sun and stopped.

People covered the station's grounds and filled the street for at least another block in both directions.

The crowd roared, whistled and clapped when the three appeared on the elevated porch of the radio station.

He waited for the noise to die down.

"I've got two amazing people I want to introduce to you in a few moments. But first, my fellow Americans, thank you all for coming out today. Maybe this can be a new beginning. Our nation has been rent and torn long enough.

But if the people will not acknowledge the rending of America, they will not have the stomach or backbone for the repairing of America. And, fellow countrymen and women, it's time to repair the United States of America."

The cheering resumed, drowning out the big speakers of the PA system.

Hunter waited until the crowd noise subsided.

"Where will we find the truths that will show us the way forward to restore our once great nation? Where should we look for that truth?

"In America, there has been so much deception that we have lost truth. Something happens when people lose truth. It's a sad condition. But it is one thing to have lost truth, and quite another to have lost the *belief* in truth. And the latter is where many find themselves in postmodern America. So, when Jesus says, "...for this reason I came into the world—to testify to the truth," we should not be surprised that so few will listen to his words ... or our words about Him. But it is precisely those words that we need desperately today.

"I'm talking about words like blessed are those who hunger and thirst for righteousness, for they will be filled.

"Blessed are the merciful, for they will be shown mercy.

"Blessed are the pure in heart: for they shall see God.

"Blessed are, not the troublemakers, but the *peacemakers*: for they shall be called the children of God.

"And beware of false prophets, which come to you in sheep's clothing, but inwardly they are ravening wolves. We've seen enough of those lately.

"Jesus' words cut to the quick, don't they? But they also separate the quick from the dead. So if we want to live in a quickened America, we must relearn the American legacy, founded on biblical principles. Then we must value it. We must live free, but without license. And come election time, we must vote accordingly, because, as I have pointed out, our benefits and rights are not guaranteed. They must be protected and handed down. May we hand them down to our children, to *my* children.

One voice rang out above the din of the crowd. "Keep on preachin', brother!"

"I intend to, sir."

The cheering started again.

If it was this loud now, what would it be like when he introduced Sam and AJ?

"Young adults, those of my generation, this is our chance. Resurrect true liberty, justice, and decency in America. Resurrect America! "

The roar from the crowd forced him to wait before continuing.

While Hunter waited, he scanned the crowd.

Moms stood with toddlers on their hips and some with another child in tow. Dads stood with kids sitting on their shoulders towering above the crowd. Older couples stood side-by-side with expectant, hopeful expressions.

The people represented every shade of the human rainbow. Like the old Sunday School song said, all precious in his sight.

This was a microcosm of America and that thought added to the adrenaline surge coursing through Hunter's veins.

It was time to continue.

"As we try to resurrect America, know this, millions of people are praying for us to do that very thing. Are you with me?"

"Yes," the crowd replied.

"I said, are you *with* me?"

"Yes!" It came louder this time.

Hunter turned to Sam and took her hand. "This is my daughter, Samantha. We call her Sam."

The crackling sound of clapping hands started but was drowned out by a spontaneous cheer from the crowd. "Sam! Sam! Sam!"

He waited for the cheer to fade.

In the distance, more people walked down the sidewalks to join the still growing audience. Thankfully, the police had blocked the street running by the radio station.

Hunter looked down at Sam beside him. "We need to hand a good and decent nation to Sam's generation, and we can start with this election."

The cheering resumed, but it faded after he took AJ's arm and pulled her beside him. "And this is AJ Scott, the best barista in the valley. Soon to be my wife, but I haven't asked her yet."

AJ socked him in the shoulder. Then leaned toward the mic. "Haven't asked me? Well, what do you intend to do about that, Hunter Jones?"

"Kiss her! Kiss her!" Public display of affection was far out of Hunter's comfort zone. But the chant wouldn't end until he complied.

"Who am I to disobey my fellow Americans?"

He kissed AJ, or was it that she kissed him? Regardless, it was a thorough job, and the response said it was a crowd-pleaser.

AJ cupped his cheeks and held his face close to hers. "Hunter, what if I had been that Amazon you thought I was?"

Hunter covered the mic before any more of this discussion went public.

"You know, six-foot-four, two-hundred-ten pounds of muscle and sinew?"

"I guess I'd still have to marry you, or you'd pound me into submission." He uncovered the mic.

"That's a rather high opinion you have of yourself, just making the assumption that I would want to marry you, that I would even try to force you to."

The crowd had grown quiet, obviously listening to their banter.

"You'd do it for Sam, because you know that nobody gets to Sam without going through me."

"That's some fancy footwork for a data analyst."

"I know you wouldn't want to disappoint Sam. So, AJ Scott, will you marry me?"

An eerie silence enveloped the entire area. Was anyone out there breathing?

Someone in the crowd coughed. It sounded like an explosion.

When the silence grew uncomfortable, AJ broke it. "Here's the deal. If you can get Zach to play *America the Beautiful*, and if Sam wants this marriage to happen—"

"I do. I do." Sam's voice blasted over the PA system as she wedged her way closer to the mic. She put one arm around AJ's waist, the other around Hunter's. "Just like I said, we can be a family."

"Okay, Sam," AJ said. "It's time for some drama. You get to lead us in your favorite song."

Zach poked Hunter in the back. "*America the Beautiful*, coming right up. Susan's in the studio and she heard."

In a few seconds, the great song opened with the trumpet fanfare.

Zach shoved a mic into Sam's hands. "It's all yours, Sam. Keep your mouth close to it. If you really belt it out, all these people will sing along with you."

The words began, sung by Ray Charles' in his distinctive baritone voice. Sam came in an octave higher, loud and strong. But her voice sounded more like a teenager than an eight- or nine-year-old girl.

The audience picked it up on the third measure.

Sam had the lead. Her face said she knew it. And her eyes said that leading a four-thousand-voice choir was an incredible power trip.

And Sam knew how to lead this song. She had memorized the Ray Charles version when she was six.

Hunter looked down into AJ's face and America grew even more beautiful.

He pulled AJ behind Sam, handed his mic to Zach, then held her snugly. "What's it going to be, Amazon Jane?"

"Did you know Jones was the most common surname in America?"

"What kind of answer is that?"

"An all-American name for an all-American time like this. I'd be glad to take your name. And, of course, Sam with it."

"Is Sam the reason you—" She muted his lips with her fingers.

"You silly data geek. How could I refuse a man who would love me sight unseen?"

AJ kissed Hunter and sealed a deal that had started with an improbable, cell-phone relationship, one that started with bickering but ended with a betrothal.

Half the crowd clapped and whistled. The rest followed Sam through the second verse of the song.

A lot of work remained, But if this crowd was any indication, they were off to a good start in winning back America.

AJ's forehead wrinkled, forming her cute frown. "Hunter, didn't they make a movie where the whole thing was about one cell phone call?"

"Yeah. Cell call or Cellular—something like that. But that story was a thriller."

"Our story was a thriller too, don't you think?"

"Yeah. I guess it was. But I don't think that cellular story ended in a marriage."

AJ's voice lowered to her sultry alto. "You know, I've heard that marriage can be pretty thrilling."

Vivid memories replayed of his first glimpse of a beautiful, slender, brown-haired woman who leaped into his truck, cheeks streaked with tears. She had fit the picture he had created in his mind during their combative phone conversations. Well, she fit the picture that had formed after Amazon Jane had been ruled out.

Now her eyes studied him, waiting for his reaction to her thrilling marriage comment.

Hunter scanned AJ's face. He drank it all in, including the shiner. He scanned a little farther taking in her shapely form.

AJ's eyes narrowed.

He smiled.

After a few seconds, she returned it.

Like Sam, she was going to be a handful.

But thrilling? How could life with a woman like AJ be anything else?

The End

If you enjoyed *Slanted*, please consider leaving a rating and a brief review on Amazon. Reviews are difficult to get and greatly appreciated by authors and readers. You can find *Slanted* on H. L. Wegley's Amazon Author Page.

Author's Notes

While researching the impacts of the suspected bias of Internet search engines, and the left-leaning IT industry as a whole, I discovered the work of Dr. Robert Epstein. Dr. Epstein is a Senior Research Psychologist at the American Institute for Behavioral Research and Technology. Based on his work, Dr. Epstein came up with a numerical estimate of the votes that were swayed by the liberal bias of the largest search engine in the world. The estimate was frightening in that, if correct, it gave more potential political power to the IT giants than to any other organization on the planet. Any possible Russian influence would have been microscopic compared to that of the search engines.

Here's a quote from Dr. Epstein, speaking of the algorithms implemented in Internet search engines. "We are looking at the power that these algorithms have to shift opinions, and there's never been anything like this in human history." Impressive but scary.

As I read Dr. Epstein's reports and interviews, the conspiracy for the plot of *Slanted* was born. Please note that I built malevolent intent into my villain, James Bratkowski. This character does not represent anyone in the IT industry or anyone I know of on the planet. He is a despicable villain that I crafted solely for my story. As with many authors, I look to find potential evil in the real world, and then I emphasize the danger by making it happen in my story.

My wife, Babe, and I grew up in Grants Pass, Oregon, about thirty miles from where the story begins, in Medford. I have aunts and uncles around Medford and cousins in Sams Valley, the home of the hero, Hunter Jones. So this is an area I know well. I've swam, fished, and rafted in the Rogue River. It's the river flowing by the park where the action in the story starts.

From Southern Oregon, the setting of *Slanted* moves to Central Oregon, east of the Cascade Mountains to La Pine and the area around Paulina Lake. Two years ago, while vacationing with Babe's two sisters, we drove up to Paulina Lake, walked through the big obsidian flow, and then drove to the top of Paulina Peak. There, at 8,000 feet on a clear summer day and from sixty miles away, I got an incredible shot of the Three Sisters, adjacent volcanic peaks in the Cascades. I'll put it up on my blog and Facebook pages for you all to see.

This area of Central Oregon is spectacular in its diversity of geography and in its beauty. So, as I often do, I chose an area of beauty to contrast it with the ugliness of man's depraved nature and his evil deeds. Using the innocence of Sam, the nearly nine-year-old girl, also added to this contrast of good and evil.

Hunter's impassioned speech near the end of the story is a composite of things I've posted in *My Two Cents for the Day* on my Facebook profile. Some of his speech may look familiar if you follow me on Facebook. Hopefully, it was inspiring, informative, and not boring. It is perhaps the most real part of this work of fiction.

I hope you enjoyed the story. While I don't think it's my best writing, *Slanted* does highlight a very real danger that all Americans need to be aware of, the power of the information we see—or are prevented from seeing—to sway our minds without us even realizing it.

To counter this, we need to teach our children well, to teach them to think critically and to separate fact from prevarication. This is perhaps the greatest need and the greatest failure of public education in America. Often, kids, even college students, are discouraged from, or punished for, attempting to think critically. That's a sad commentary on public education and on academia.

At the end of the story, my characters mention a movie, *Cellular*. It was a thriller about a jeopardized cell call on which the lives of all members of one family depended. That plot gave me the idea for AJ and Hunter building a relationship over the phone before their first meeting, an event that didn't take place until halfway through the story.

If you enjoyed *Slanted*, look for another action-packed, romantic suspense story with thriller-level stakes in late 2019. In the meantime, please check out my other books. They're all listed on my Amazon author page: https://amzn.to/2jnQSYt

H. L. Wegley

Don't miss H. L. Wegley's award-winning, political-thriller series, with romance, *Against All Enemies*:

Book 1: Voice in the Wilderness

Book 2: Voice of Freedom

Book 3: Chasing Freedom (The Prequel)

Read all three books in the *Witness Protection Series*—action and romance with thriller-level stakes—clean reads that are never graphic, gratuitous, or gross.

This series can be read in any order.

No Turning Back

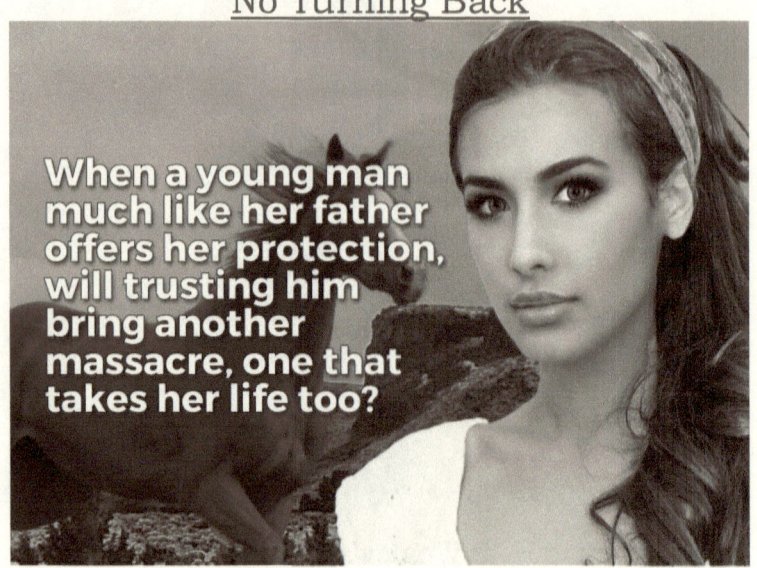

Witness Protection Series

Book 1: No Safe Place

Book 2: No True Justice

Book 3: No Turning Back

Romantic suspense with thriller-level stakes
For recent college graduate, Alisa (Allie)
Petrenko, the Cold War never ended, and events
set in motion years ago have endangered this
innocent young woman. When her father is
murdered, he left her with a warning, an
assassin on her trail, and his secret history
contained in a set of journals. As Allie tries to
elude the assassin and read the journals, she
learns that the loving father who raised her was
not the man he appeared to be, and the man she
must now trust with her life is someone Allie
must never trust with her heart.

The Janus Journals